VIETNAM

BOOK FIVE

WALKING WOUNDED

CHRIS LYNCH

SCHOLASTIC INC.

If you purchased this book without a cover, you should be aware that this book is stolen property. It was reported as "unsold and destroyed" to the publisher, and neither the author nor the publisher has received any payment for this "stripped book."

Copyright © 2014 by Chris Lynch

This book was originally published in hardcover by Scholastic Press in 2014.

All rights reserved. Published by Scholastic Inc., *Publishers since 1920*. SCHOLASTIC and associated logos are trademarks and/or registered trademarks of Scholastic Inc.

The publisher does not have any control over and does not assume any responsibility for author or third-party websites or their content.

No part of this publication may be reproduced, stored in a retrieval system, or transmitted in any form or by any means, electronic, mechanical, photocopying, recording, or otherwise, without written permission of the publisher. For information regarding permission, write to Scholastic Inc., Attention: Permissions Department, 557 Broadway, New York, NY 10012.

This book is a work of fiction. Names, characters, places, and incidents are either the product of the author's imagination or are used fictitiously, and any resemblance to actual persons, living or dead, business establishments, events, or locales is entirely coincidental.

ISBN 978-0-545-64016-9

10 9 8 7 6 5 4 3 2 1   16 17 18 19 20

Printed in the U.S.A.   40
First printing 2016

The text type was set in Sabon MT.
Book design by Christopher Stengel

PART
ONE

Ivan

It has to stop somewhere.

It looks like it's just gonna go on and on and on, but that would be such a nightmare, it's the kind of nightmare that nightmares have nightmares about. It has to stop somewhere. Somebody's got to do something.

This war, or some version of it, seems to have been going on for centuries. Nobody has had any success in ending it over all that time, and I see no indication that anybody is going to manage any differently any time soon.

Somebody's got to.

So it looks like it's up to me. If nobody else is going to do what needs to be done, then I will.

CHAPTER TWO

Morris

I am the one who will take Rudi home.

Normal protocol regarding body escorts is that somebody from the same unit as the deceased is put on the detail. Meaning, in this case, somebody other than me.

Absolutely, over-my-dead-body no.

"Sir," I say to the officer in charge, "I have a request."

The officer has seen a lot, as everybody here has seen a lot, so despite the urgency in my voice he's slow in raising his head from his paperwork. When finally, lazily, he does, he goes wide-eyed as he takes in the sight of me from brain to boots.

It does give me a small thrill to see his expression. It is nearly impossible to get anything but bombed-out boredom from these guys these days.

"Sure, pal," he says in a nearly human voice. "What d'ya need?"

He is still sizing me up all over even as he politely struggles to pretend that he is not, that he is processing me just the same as every other faceless slob asking for his grace in this graceless situation.

Except, of course, I'm not faceless. I have a face, and it is lacquered in my old pal Rudi's truest, bluest, red blood. I feel the blood trickling down my features and puddling in the hollow of my collarbone. I see my hands, soaked in Rudi, look at my uniform, drenched in Rudi, and I wonder how I even got here, to this man, who makes these decisions.

Beck is still there, right now. I left him with Rudi. With the remains of Rudi. For all I know, he's still trying to revive the poor dope. Even though we know he's gone. Even though we probably knew he was gone from the moment we saw him.

Smart guys like Beck should know better. You would expect them to know better. You would expect the pathetic, mushy types like me to be back there on that trail trying to stanch the blood flowing out of the hopeless body, trying to breathe the kiss of life back into the life that's already kissed us good-bye.

But there you go. You would expect, and you would be wrong. I got straight up, left Rudi in the warm embrace of Beck, and simply knew there was one thing to do now, one thing that mattered more than every other possible thing.

I had to take Rudi home.

It was *my* pledge, for the love of God. My pledge that brought us here. I forced everybody into this, and the idea was that we were going to look after each other. We were going to look after Rudi.

We failed at that. We did worse, even.

"I need to be the body escort seeing a particular fallen Marine home," I say.

"I'm sure we can do that," the officer says, happy to look away from me and back to his stack of sheets of human statistics. "Name of Marine?"

I give it to him.

"I'm sorry," he says after a long and increasingly desperate troll through the stats. He does, in fact, sound truly sorry. "We don't have any casualties by that name reported."

I open my mouth and prepare to shout at him because, really, shouting at somebody in a position like his might feel pretty good right now. Then I realize it's the opposite. Shouting at this man would feel obscene to me just at this moment.

I hold out my arms instead. I see them glistening with all the wrong things.

Who ever would have thought that one hole in that brain could have produced all that blood?

"He won't have been reported yet," I say softly. "But he's here, if you want verification. And here and here and here."

I hold out my weary and blood-sodden arms for as long as I can manage it. The officer seems to notice my struggle as my arms sink lower and lower and I foolishly try to hold on.

He reaches out, seizes my putrid, decaying-Rudi wrists, and forces me to lower my arms back to my sides.

"You will see your friend home," he says. "Every step of the journey. I promise I will see to it."

CHAPTER THREE

Beck

Morris couldn't take it.

Which is fine. Who could take this? How would you even learn to take something like this? You can't. And that's why you only discover how you'll do when you are forced to do.

Morris couldn't take it, so he just up and left. He got up, a bloody and crying mess, and staggered away down the trail that leads to the base. He must have passed the jeep that's now tearing up that trail toward me. Toward us. Rudi and me.

The medics realize in less than a second that there is nothing they can do for the boy. So, gently but insistently, they pry him out of my grip. I think we must have looked like that sculpture of Mary holding the body of Jesus, the *Pietà*. Then, as the body of Rudi rises in front of me, lifted away by the medics, I see dangling around his neck, with his dog tags, the scapular. The little cloth image of Jesus that Rudi got from Ivan's parents. To protect him from harm.

Couldn't protect him from Ivan, though.

Rudi is stretchered across the back of the jeep as it barrels back down the trail, and I sit there with him, holding him in place so he doesn't go bouncing out and onto the ground. That would be just like him.

I helped him pass his tests back in school, so he could keep up and stay with us.

The medic at the wheel drives with a sense of urgency that strikes me as bizarre since Rudi is in less of a hurry than he has ever been. Time doesn't mean much.

The jeep skids to a stop in front of the base's medical building, and I follow silently behind as the medics carry the stretcher through the doors, across the main ward with a dozen variously mangled soldiers who salute to the best of their abilities as we pass, and out another door at the far end.

I guess you would call this the morgue. There are four tables, two of them supporting bodies that are covered in sheets. One is empty. One is now Rudi's rest.

The medics salute me, which they don't have to do and which makes me feel childishly better about things.

Then they leave, and I am alone. With Rudi and two strange man-shaped sheets.

Is that alone? I'd say, probably.

I stare at his stupid little face there and almost smile when I realize that, despite the sick pallor and the gruesome hole at his temple and the general obscene mess of him, he looks like Rudi. He looks like the Rudi we knew in Boston. He looks more like himself than he did the last time we saw him alive.

"What am I going to tell your ma?" I ask the little dope as he lies there all emptied. "What am I going to tell *all* the mas? And the dads." I think about my own father, his horror and disgust over this whole conflict even before this. I think about . . . Jeez. I think about Ivan's dad. What will this do to The Captain? "No parting words for me, Rude? Isn't there some wisdom that comes with death that you could pass on, huh? Look at this, kid, *me* asking *you* for wisdom. Probably not likely to happen again, so you should probably take advantage."

I wait a few seconds, because I guess when it comes down to it, in a moment like this, I am just as foolish and hopeful as any true believer who wastes time praying for stuff he'll never get.

Ultimately, Rudi does take the opportunity to lay

his wisdom-of-the-dead on me. By lying there quiet, broken, and bloodless.

"Right, pal," I say, and scoot my chair up close to his bedside. I lean forward and lay my head on his chest, on ribs almost certainly cracked by Morris's maniacal efforts at resuscitation.

I listen, foolishly, for the dead heart to thump again, but I hear something else, a voice from behind me: "I'm taking him home."

I keep my head resting on Rudi.

"Did you hear me, Beck?" Morris says. "I said I'm taking Rudi home."

"I think he's already as home as he's going to get."

"Yeah, well, I'm delivering him to his real home, in Boston. I'm his body escort."

I lift my head to look at Morris. My hand rests on Rudi's chest as I do. It's almost as difficult to look at the old pal standing upright as the old pal on the slab. Morris's face looks just as drained of blood as Rudi's. Except, of course, where Morris's face is *wearing* Rudi's blood.

"You have a little somebody on your face there," I say, pointing at my own face like you do when you try to point out a spot of food.

"You do that joking thing if you have to, Beck. . . ."

I have to. "I'll stop."

"The officer in charge is arranging it, for me to body escort."

"That's where you went? To arrange that?"

"Yeah."

"That was pretty quick thinking. I'm impressed."

"I'm not sure if I was thinking at all. Just found myself doing it."

"The good old subconscious. It always knows what it's doing, even when we don't."

Morris grins at that, looks down at the floor, then up again. He gestures toward my hand on Rudi. "Any miracles in the cards? How's he doing?"

My turn to grin. "A little sluggish."

We linger for a minute on the laugh. The last of probably a billion the three of us shared. The four of us shared.

Morris's already big softy eyes go all bleary and teary. "Maybe you should come along with us," he says.

I shake my head. "Nah. They'll never let it happen. And I have a job to do. I'm happy enough knowing you'll be with him. Awful to think of him traveling all that way, in that box, all alone."

That makes him worse, and he snuffles along through it. "Wouldn't be alone anyway," he says.

"There's always somebody for an escort, even if it's somebody who didn't know him."

My subconscious decides this is a good time to be rubbing Rudi's chest the way you would a good dog's belly.

"That would be alone," I say. "Nobody knew him. Just the three of us."

The three of us.

"What are we gonna do, Beck?" Morris asks, on the pleading side of asking. He walks over to us now, pulls a chair to the other side of the table, and puts a hand alongside my hand on Rudi.

"We're going to wait for the doc, who's going to come in and look the boy over. Then he's going to write up the form that declares that little Rudi is truly gone. That the cause of death was a single, perfect sniper's bullet to the head."

Perfect sniper's bullet.

"But then? What are we gonna do after that?"

"Well, my experience having one of my friends shoot another one of my friends is pretty limited. But I'm thinking, after that, you're going to take a trip home with our poor pal and I'm going to report back for duty."

It's Morris's turn to lay his head down on the kid.

That rib cage has had to withstand a lot in death. Though not nearly what it absorbed in life.

"Beck?" Morris says in a whisper of a wounded moan.

The doctor pushes through the door.

"After that, I don't know," I say. "We'll just have to get to *after that* after that."

"Excuse me, men," says the doctor, who is all busy and all business. He gently and coldly removes my hand and all of Morris from the body so he can do his thing and be done with it.

See ya, Rudi, pal.

I put my arm around Morris as we head for the exit, and he puts his arm around me. He can't stop looking back, and we nearly do the old Three Stooges stuck-in-a-doorway routine as I manhandle him out of the morgue.

CHAPTER FOUR

Ivan

I catch a ride with a convoy of Army Engineers heading south on Route 1 from Chu Lai to Qui Nhon. The weather is balmy and I feel like I want to be outside for the rest of my life, so I'm perfectly content to jump in the back of this big, dirty transport vehicle and nestle in the dirt watching the sky go by.

They are transporting some rich and aromatic soil for whatever creative weirdness the Engineers are up to this time. It makes a comfortable nest for me.

It's busy here, I realize as I watch vehicles pass us regularly. It's busy on the road and it sure is busy in the thickets of trees that line the route.

It reminds me of Route 93, which my dad and I used to take up into New Hampshire to the little cabin there. Just the two of us, and a lot of quiet country and shooting. I loved those hunting trips with my dad.

I watch all those trees and think of all the Vietcong who have set up in there to kill Americans over these last few years. We should have snipers like me on every truck, in every vehicle, riding shotgun up and down each major route in Vietnam, picking off every assassin out there. That would work. Then we could leave this place. We could all go home.

It should be harder to kill people than it is. But it's so easy. Only the afterward is hard.

CHAPTER FIVE

Morris

The duty officer, Daniels, is a man true to his word.

You would think it would be a pretty rational and straightforward thing. I was visiting Rudi in Chu Lai. I had known him forever. I was pumping his chest as he died. You would think that I would be given the body-escort assignment without even needing to ask for it.

You would think. If you were never in the US Armed Services, you would think that to be the reasonable conclusion.

But, after five miles of red tape, we are almost there. One significant hurdle remains. It had not immediately occurred to me that I would have to clear the assignment with my own commanding officer. There is no good reason why this had not immediately occurred to me, since that is precisely the way the Navy works, but recent events have possibly affected my thinking.

"Your CO wants to talk to you," Daniels says as I walk into his office. I am all showered up but have gotten right back into the awful clothes I had on when Rudi got splattered all over me. On Daniels's desk is a sharp new set of proper Navy dress gear. He points at it and nods at me as he hands me the phone and leaves.

"Captain?" I say.

"Are you well, private?" he says.

"I'm . . . okay, cap. Thanks for asking."

"I got your request."

I don't say anything because I can't think of what I'm expected to say.

"Are you there?"

"Yes, captain."

"Okay, to the point. I am very sorry about your friend."

"Thank you. I really —"

"But you know, *everybody's* best friend is dying here. It doesn't stop them from doing their duty."

Oh. Oh, no, no.

"Sir, I'm sorry. I understand. It's just, this is important. It's a special case. There was this pledge we all made to stay together, and I forced that on —"

"You realize there is only seven weeks left on your tour."

"What?" I say, confused by the turn of the conversation, oblivious to this or any other statistic right now that does not involve me and Rudi and a long, long trip. "Uh, no, sir. But this won't take too long. I won't spend any more time there than absolutely necessary to see things right, to talk to Rudi's . . . and my . . ."

"Well, it will take some time."

"Please, cap. You have to let me." I have picked up the fresh uniform and am cradling it like some fragile creature I'm trying to keep alive with my will and hope and not much else.

"Calm down, son. I'm letting you go."

"Thank you, captain. Thank you. I'll make sure you won't regret this, and I'll get the job done and turn around and be back before you hardly know I'm away."

"Well, no," he says calmly.

"No? Captain? No?"

"No. No, I won't regret it, and no, you won't be back."

My heart starts beating like chopper blades, and I wonder how much more of this it can take.

"You're losing me, sir."

He lets out a small, sharp laugh. "Well, yes, precisely. Son, for the last several weeks you've spent more time on the radio trying to arrange this family reunion of yours than you have on anything else. Since the day we lost Moses, in fact, you haven't been much good to me. I've been worried you are going to get yourself killed and maybe the rest of us, too. I need a full complement of fighting men, and frankly, at this stage, you are not one."

That's right, I'm not. I never wanted to be one. That's not why I came.

"I'm sorry, cap," I say, feeling embarrassment but not much else.

"Don't be sorry. Just escort your friend home, and then stay there. I've put in the request. I'm still awaiting a response but I told them everything I just told you. Between that and your short-time status, nobody else is going to want you, either. This will go through. You'll be rotated back to stateside duty, yet to be determined."

I have never been so humiliated and ecstatic in my life.

"Thank you for everything, captain."

"Take care of yourself, private. And have a good life."

We hang up. I stand there with the clothes in my hand, looking back and forth from them to the phone and back again.

I'm going home.

We're going home.

CHAPTER SIX

Ivan

Lieutenant?"

I hear the voice, sounding distant and very close at the same time.

"Lieutenant? Is there something I should know here?"

I almost look behind me to see who he might be talking to when I remember I'm a second lieutenant. As my confirmed kills rose, so did my field promotions, to the point where my CO said I should reach major general before my tour is over.

I roll over, from my side onto my back. There is rich soil all over the side of my face and over much of my head. I sit up. I am covered in the stuff, as if the motion of the truck has been tossing me around, or as if I have myself been thrashing and wallowing like a mad barnyard animal.

At the open end of the truck there's an officer looking at me strangely. "What's this all about?" he says, pointing at a spot to my left.

I look over and see that he is pointing at my deadly M-21 Sniper Weapon System, assembled and poised and extended through the mesh cage of the truck.

He had been unaware that his truck was actually a mobile sniper's nest.

"Just trying to pay my way, sir," I say as I scramble up and start taking the gun apart. "Riding shotgun, providing cover for the convoy along the route."

I have the full system broken down and back in its canvas carrier before he can even respond.

"Uh-huh," he says, unmoved. "Who knows what kind of bandits might have stolen all our dirt if you weren't there sleeping on it."

"Ha," I say, hopping down off the tail of the truck and walking on past him.

"That's a special weapon there," he says.

"It is," I say, walking faster.

"You must be a talent."

"I never miss. Thanks for the lift."

"Our pleasure."

At the base at Qui Nhon I hook up with another, smaller convoy hauling supplies of ammunition and building materials along Highway 19 to Pleiku. This is about half the distance we covered on Route 1, but it will be much less of a highway trip and more of a grind.

This stretch between the port and the Central Highlands has become famous for being the rope pulled taut in a tug-of-war between us and them. The VC have used it to get men and supplies to their million little hideaways between here and Cambodia and beyond. Then we have fought to take it violently away from them. Then they have come back to destroy the road and bridges in strategic spots to make life hell for us, and we have rebuilt the road and the bridges to get back to business and make life hell for them.

I couldn't even tell you which side has the upper hand in the endless battle for Highway 19 as I hop aboard the convoy that's about to travel it.

But I do know that this convoy includes the brute-beast gun trucks that the last one did not.

And I also know that a stretch of Highway 19 is helpfully referred to as Ambush Alley.

The convoy contains around one hundred vehicles altogether, sent out in staggered groups of ten. I am in the second group, embarking ten minutes after the first.

I've gotten myself onto one of the gun trucks. There is one assigned to each group. The gun truck is actually a converted five-ton cargo vehicle, but its similarity with the rest of the cargo haulers ends with the name. It is surrounded with steel plates on three sides and below, and the bed in back is modified beyond all recognition. There are two men stationed up top behind .50-caliber machine guns, and one grenadier manning an M-79 grenade launcher. This is serious firepower for a haulage convoy, and a direct response to all the damage Charlie has done to us along this route.

The mood is as tense and serious as on any assignment I have been on so far. We are the third truck in the second convoy, and every man is on high alert from the moment we set out.

The road is terrible. It's rutted and pocked and only sporadically paved. I lean over the side of the truck to get a look at what's out there when I feel us slide sideways for the third time. The road widens and narrows without any apparent pattern, and once we start the climb into the hills it becomes obvious that we could tumble off the road and down the side of a mountain without needing much of a shove.

"Can I have a look?" one of the two machine

gunners says, motioning toward the canvas bag that holds my weapon.

I stare at him for a few seconds, looking at his hard face, his long arm stuck out in the direction of my gun as if I really didn't have any say in the matter.

Crrrack. Ping.

It's sniper fire. The first shot ricochets off the steel plating right between me and the presumptuous gunner guy, and everybody jumps right in. Both .50s roar to life and fill the hill above us with blanket fire. The M-79 launches a grenade into the side of the hill and the explosion brings rocks rumbling down to crash into the truck running behind us.

I have my rifle out and ready in seconds, and I crouch in position behind the plate and watch for muzzle fire while the rest of these boys fire away wildly.

I'm thinking about the waste. About the rounds and rounds of ammo being drilled into the ground to no effect, when we are risking our lives in this convoy to deliver more ammunition to more of our soldiers, who are going to eventually do the same thing with it.

What are we doing here?

"What are you waiting for? Shoot!" the grenadier shouts.

I ignore him and wait another several seconds and then there is another *crrrack* and *ping* and a muzzle flash high up on the hill, and I scope and I line him up, even in the bumpy back of a rumbling gun truck, and we all see the vicious little killer fall right down out of that tree sticking out of that bluff and crash down that rocky hillside and keep crashing 'til he is stopped dead by a rock as big as this truck. Somebody reaches over amid the hollering and pats my shoulder, and I smack that hand away hard enough to maybe send a few fingers spinning off into the countryside, and then there is another muzzle flash and I aim and the beautiful clean *bang* of my M-21 is in the air and another VC assassin is out of another tree and tumbling down when we turn a big bend in the road and ride out of that particular skirmish.

"Holy smokes," the grenadier says, crouching down to look at — but not touch — my rifle. "Who are you, soldier?"

"From a moving vehicle under extreme circumstances," says one gunner.

"Two confirmed kills," says the other gunner, "within, what, half a minute?"

I am rechecking the gun, wiping it down, cleaning the scope, which is already dusty from this awful road.

"How many?" the grenadier asks, and we all know what he is referring to.

Everybody wants the number.

I cannot give it to them.

I look up, at the one guy, then the other, then the other.

And I give them a 100-percent truthful shrug.

CHAPTER SEVEN

Morris

This is how it goes," Daniels says the following day, when all the other preparations have been made for both Rudi and me. We are on the strip at Chu Lai Airfield, just under and behind the wing of the C-123 transport plane. Marines are busy loading cargo into the gut of the aircraft, while Rudi lies in his box on a gurney between Daniels and me.

Snap, snap, snap, snap.

"Are you listening to me, kid? Because what I am telling you are not just suggestions. They are how it *has to go*. Even more than battlefield orders, these rules absolutely must be carried out no matter what it takes, and you are solely responsible for making sure that they are."

"Sorry, sir," I say, aware now that I was paying attention to Rudi when I should have been paying attention to orders. I was staring down at his steel-gray box, which contains a gray steel box, which contains the remains. I'm still trying to align it all in my head, but it won't settle.

"We treat this duty as way beyond sacred. We treat it as if it is us in that box, and how we feel like we should be handled."

I wish it were me in there instead. I wouldn't care how I was handled.

But Rudi deserves more, and I get it.

"He gets on the plane feetfirst. Not negotiable. Then, it's a cargo plane, so there's cargo. I don't care how loaded it is, *nothing* goes on top of him. Right?"

"Right."

"You will change aircraft, possibly multiple times. I don't care who is on duty, you stay right there with our comrade. Right?"

"Right." I get a little more barky with each affirmation.

"When he is loaded up, and when he's placed in the hold, his head is always down. Why is his head always down?"

I was not expecting anything like a quiz on this.

"Because . . . he's been defeated?" I say.

Pathetic. I am embarrassed by the lameness of my answer, but for a fleeting moment I'm also amused.

That was such a Rudi response that I could almost believe it was him taking over and talking through me.

My shoulders shiver. I need to stop that kind of thinking if I am going to see this particular duty through.

"Because," Daniels somehow growls warmly, "he has been embalmed, and if the fluid flows away from his head and to his feet he will start decomposing before he gets all the way home. That is bad, any way you look at it, but it is particularly bad if the folks back home want to have an open casket and have a last look at this brave soldier. Do you suppose —"

"Yes, sir, I do."

"Good. Then you will appreciate the importance of following these rules like a tenacious guard dog defending his master."

"Sir, I will follow these rules, in just that fashion."

Like Rudi should have been guarded all along.

The C-123's engines cough and bark and then roar to life. The twin propellers beat the air with a *pap-pap-pap* authority that instantly makes all but essential personnel flee the scene.

Daniels gives me a salute.

Nobody has ever had to salute me before. It makes me crack a little, makes me feel important, because I suppose it makes Rudi important. And who was ever going to predict that before this whole thing started?

Daniels backs away and leaves it to me.

It really is mine now, the responsibility, the *care* of this poor simple kid. I thought he was in my care all along. I kidded myself. I lied.

The Marines who have loaded the plane seem to believe it now, though, because as the engines roar to life and they finish with their cargo, they march over in formation and in respect and stop in front of Rudi and me, and they wait.

They wait for me to give them the signal, because until I do, nobody is going anywhere.

Because we all know it could just as well be us. And because it goes just like this, because this is the right way to treat him.

I am about to give them the signal to load my boy, my pal, my sadness and my guilt, onto the plane for the final journey, when I see somebody passing Daniels on his way to this spot. And I wait.

We all wait, because it seems like we should. Nobody moves 'til he gets here.

"That was my aircraft," Beck says, shouldering right up against me, facing the scene with me.

"Was it, now?" I say.

"Yes, sir. Modified, of course," he says. "It was a Provider, Ranch Hand. I sprayed so much Agent Orange out of this thing I'll defoliate every garden in Boston just by walking past."

I nod, laugh a little.

"But I did it for him. And for Ivan. Cleared those banks of that foliage so the VC couldn't hide and kill our boys. That's why I did that awful thing."

"I know," I say. "The same reason I did all of what I did, off the coast and up all those scary Mekong river-ways. For them, pal. We did everything for them."

"Because them was us."

"And us was them."

"And look where it got everybody. Look how they thank us."

Bless their souls, the Marines know nothing about what we are talking about yet they remain rigid monuments all the while.

"We won't look at it today, though," I say.

"No, sir," Beck says, and he takes it upon himself to salute Rudi and begin the good-bye for good.

Now he's done it.

"Oh, man . . . ," I say, joining in the salute and triggering the orderly action of the Marines carefully shouldering one of their own. "I'm supposed to be in charge here," I say softly as Beck and I hold our salutes and I completely wash my own face with the crying.

"You're doing fine," he says.

"Feetfirst," I croak, with no hope of them hearing me.

"It's good, don't worry. They know what they're doing."

"And they have to load him so his head is in the right position, because —"

"They'll give him a pillow, I'm sure."

As Rudi slides into the belly of the C-123, Beck and I release our salutes. As we do, I hear — and I realize that for Beck this really is the final one —

"Bye, Rudi, pal," he says.

I can only guess what I look like because when he turns to face me he gets all urgent. "Come on now, Morris," he says, grabbing my shoulders firmly. "Come on now."

"I don't know how I'm going to get through all this, Beck, man."

"You're going to get through it the same way you have always gotten through everything. By being a good man, Morris, man. And by focusing on home. You're going *home*."

"Yeah, well, right now, home feels a lot scarier even

than this place does. And this place is a certified nightmare."

"It won't be bad at all, once you're in Boston, with all your people around."

"You think?"

"I do."

"Wanna trade, then?"

He releases his grip on my shoulders and tugs me by the arm toward the plane.

"Not on your life, old friend," he says with only a little pop of a laugh.

The loading crew have all jumped down and the cargo door is secured with a slam. I look through the small window as Beck stands there all alone, watching us taxi. Watching with his studious Beck brand of solitary mourning while Rudi and I take off for home and whatever that is now.

And I cannot help thinking about Ivan, where he is and what he is at this, *this* moment of ours.

CHAPTER EIGHT

Ivan

I belong in the highlands.

I have known that from the moment I arrived in Pleiku. Check that. I knew it before I arrived, when that first chopper rose out of the swampy, untrustworthy lowlands and the terrain kept on rising with us, as if to meet us. This is the geography of the hunter, the wild and irregular mountains with caves and nooks, notches and valleys and forests. It's a world that repays seriousness, attention to detail, patience, controlled anger, focus. Self-reliance.

In spite of the chaotic circumstances, this feels like coming home now. My heart rate slows. There are worse places to die.

We have been fired upon with increasing frequency as we've climbed Highway 19, and we expect more as we approach our base at An Khe. The first group has taken the brunt, and already we have passed two of their trucks — abandoned, upended, and burning off the side of the road. As the altitude has increased, so has the caliber of ordnance being thrown at us. Rocket-propelled grenades took out those trucks, and one almost got us, sailing right past and into the hillside between us and the next vehicle in line. It's become clear from the heads-down dash of the operation that nobody expects the full convoy to reach Pleiku. Everybody involved seems to understand it's just a big brutal game of *red rover, red rover*, except if you fail to ram through you don't get to just join hands with the other team.

We run into another barrage about a mile from An Khe. Mortar rounds come surging up out of the dense greenery that runs all down along the slopes of Hon Cong Mountain, and for about two minutes it is furious.

"There's nothing even to shoot at!" one gunner screams out from a crouching position. Mortar shells are landing all around us. The road just ahead suddenly erupts in a great *boom*, and a plume of smoke and rock and earth sweeps over us as we barrel and bang over the crater at full speed. Us guys up here on the gun truck's top deck are thrown all over but scramble right back into place.

"Well, shoot at it anyway!" the other gunner screams.

They do indeed blast away, down the slope, while trying to remain largely behind the truck's steel plating. The grenadier lobs away in the general direction of the mortar nests and doesn't even pretend to strain for visual contact.

Such a waste.

"You don't just shoot for the noise of it!" I shout through the commotion.

"*You* don't even shoot for that," one gunner snaps back.

"That's right, I don't," I say. I'm sitting with my back to the armored wall, my knees up to stabilize me. I take the cloth I've been using to keep all this dirt and debris from compromising my rifle, and I mop the sweat that's started running heavily down my face. It's blood, though, I see now. Sweat, too, lots of that. But a fair amount of blood is staining the cloth. I probably smacked my forehead on the steel plating during that last eruption, which underscores how our means of protection can cut both ways when the battle gets hot.

"Friendly fire," I say, laughing to myself when I see the blood taking over the rag on the second and third dabbing.

Except it's not a laugh. It just sounds similar to one. It doesn't have a name of its own.

There is, reasonably enough, a lull as the route passes close by An Khe itself. There is a pretty substantial base there, Camp Radcliff, which is the home of a lot of US muscle, including the 1st Air Cavalry. The relatively modest-sized opposition slinging junk at us so far wouldn't stand up to what's on offer up at the camp. Not that the North Vietnamese regulars and the Vietcong couldn't, wouldn't, and *haven't* brought the almighty wrath to these bases from the very beginning. But when they do, it's an *operation*, lasts for months, and is impossible not to notice from a very long way away.

Right now, though, the only thing Camp Radcliff means to us is a short breather while we reel in all the millions of nerve endings that have been swollen and extended and electrified enough to leave us fairly exhausted for a "noncombat operation."

We don't, however, stop moving. The trucks keep on barreling along the treacherous and unsympathetic road, and my admiration for the drivers has multiplied manyfold since I mounted this thing.

And I was just hitching a ride. I laugh. This time, it's a laugh.

"Hey, that's a Purple Heart, right there," the

grenadier says, pointing at my head. They are all sitting now around the square of the plated platform.

I bring the rag down and examine it. It's already much less out of control.

"I'm coagulating, that's the main thing," I say.

He shakes his head at me like I'm daffy or something. Then he goes into a metal supply box welded to the floor in the corner. He roots around, pulls out some gear, and approaches me.

He has a better rag than I have, and a bottle of alcohol. He peels my rancid old rag down and tosses it over the side. He splashes alcohol all over the wound and mops it out hard enough to remove any gunk, but gently enough not to restart mad bleeding. Then he's bumping my head with small punches as he plasters a big, thick bandage up there while the truck pitches and jumps around.

"I'd say about a dozen stitches," he says as he applies long strips of tape, affixing the bandage to my skull. He sits back on his haunches to admire his craftwork.

I reach up and feel it. Could be professional. It's hard like a splint, dry, and securely fixed.

"Nah," I say. "Seems like you gave it all it needs. I'm a fast healer, anyway."

"Jeez," one of the gunners says, laughing.

"I know," the other adds. "Just take your Purple Heart already."

I shake my head to indicate *no*, and to test its soundness at the same time.

"Purple Heart's for combat injury suffered in a combat situation, in a combat unit," I say like I am the regulation book itself, made man. The straightness I feel in my face nearly makes me want to laugh.

The three of them stare like I am in a zoo and they cannot make out what species I am.

"And?" the grenadier asks. "So?"

"First," I say, "I'm not even here. Officially. I'm just a hippie bum hitchhiker snagging a free ride. And second . . . C'mon, fellas. Pedaling up and down this hill delivering groceries is hardly a combat unit in a combat situation."

It seems, somehow, as if even the prodigious sounds of the engines straining and the trucks shaking and banging to pieces have ceased all at once. My three nameless hosts — because what do their names matter? — stare at me the way I know Charlie stares at me from beyond his range when I've just executed his pal for coming within mine.

Snipers live to breathe this tension right here.

"Heroic," I say coolly, and with a salute to one and two and three.

"What?" asks the multiskilled anonymous grenade-slinger from the United States Army's 8th Transportation Group.

"I said *heroic*," I am pleased to resay. "As in, that was heroic of you. I was winding you up, just to see if you'd snap. You know, like the real fighters in this war seem to do all the time."

I am pretty certain I see all three of them reach, in the O.K. *Corral* sense of the term, before I hold up both hands in the *Whoa there, pardner* sense.

I'm not even sure I'm enjoying this. And I'm not sure that I'm not. Fairly certain it is dangerous, though, which is all right.

"Okay," I say. "I'll stop now," I say. "The only way I could even play with you like that in the first place is because I know better from my own two eyes and I can respect what it is you do. You transport boys are a whole other kind of hero, and I mean that. Only wish I appreciated you more all along. I wonder how many more kinds are out there, because before, I thought there was just me."

"A *lot*. There are a *lot* more," one gunner says,

rolling back up to his station. The second does likewise without saying anything.

"What's *wrong* with you, man?" the grenadier asks me. Only he doesn't ask it in the usual way, the timeless way, the way I have asked friends and foes all my life without thinking about it.

He asks it in a way like he wants an answer. Like he's trying to get at an actual explanation for whatever it is that is gnawing at him.

He stays hovering in front of me for a bit as if he truly expects me to enlighten him. As if the question itself wasn't all the answer he needed.

In all my life I never asked it like that, no matter if I asked my best friend or my second-best friend or a nobody on the street, and it's chilling me. I never used those words in that way, no matter how many thousand times I used them, no matter how strange the other person was to make me ask the question, no matter how smart, no matter how stupid, how lost or peculiar or sad.

That was not the way those words in that arrangement were supposed to function.

Bu-hooom!

We are rocked three times as hard as at any time yet. And it is not even a hit to our group. Somewhere in the column behind us, in the next group, or the one after, an extraordinary explosion has gone off. We all look back in that direction to see the huge cone of fire and smoke and ash and airborne debris as if there were an active volcano on the road that we just happened to not notice before.

"They got at least one of the ammo trucks," one of the guys calls out.

"At least three, I'd say," somebody else yells.

We haven't come under direct fire yet, but we are all up and rigid with readiness. I have my rifle primed and ready to do whatever damage circumstances permit, though I know it wouldn't appear to be much.

I will make it count, whatever comes.

Bu-hooom!

This one is up in the group ahead. The lead bunch have taken a consistent battering, and while this explosion does not match the sheer spectacle of the last one, it seems to explode in a more focused, concentrated manner that could be all the more trouble.

We rumble on in an almost eerily unmolested fashion, skirmishes audible in every direction while we feel not a pinprick.

It nearly feels worse. At least fighting back at a thing that is coming at you is clearly a fight. Feeling nothing but the expectation leaves you sweating, twitching, vibrating to no useful effect.

It is the very worst way for a warrior to feel. You anticipate away all your vital nastiness. Then when you need it, it's spent.

If so, you get what you deserve.

I am perched high and leaning far out over the lip of the armor, trying to get a sense of the where and the what of what's out there waiting for us. But it tires of waiting and comes to visit instead.

Schwoom!

A missile flies past the right side of the truck so close it manages to boil my eyeballs with the heat, and slams spectacularly into the truck two places back. Immediately, the truck blows every which way, the main section careening into the ditch off the left side of the track while cargo and chunks of metal and man go airborne and down the mountain to the right. The flaming chassis scorches a trail across the grasses to where it slams against the rocky base of the hill.

Before it struck, the missile sounded like no other ordnance I had ever heard. It sounded like an F-4 Phantom jet, if you could get one to strafe that close to your head.

And it brought me back.

In a way I would not have anticipated, the missile has pulled me back together and into my correct condition.

I'm in danger, but I'm not in a panic. Who wouldn't take that deal every time?

CHAPTER NINE

Morris

We haven't spent this much time together since high school.

We're flying from Chu Lai to Da Nang. Da Nang to Tokyo. Tokyo to Honolulu. Honolulu to Norton Air Force Base in San Bernardino, California.

At Da Nang I learn that Rudi was actually wise to get himself killed on his own base.

"Nice and tidy," says Lieutenant Grafe, a staff officer at the Da Nang mortuary who looks even younger than me. He's boarded our plane to check that Rudi's identification and follow-on details are all in order, and to inform me I'll be escorting two more unfortunates as far as Tokyo. He checks over the paperwork, hands it back to me, and smiles in an unexpectedly friendly way. "Your comrade here did himself a clever favor by going down right there on the home court."

"Yeah," I say, "he was always good like that, with the clever planning."

"What I mean is, I get guys in here every day in every state of dishevelment. Straight from the field, planes, choppers, jeeps, some with no prep at all, no identification. We are set up to process about three hundred and fifty bodies a month through this facility and it is always a real test to get it all done, done right, and done with the proper attention to each deserving individual. And man, after Tet, we were doing more like a thousand a month. We do a fine job, but c'mon, everybody, *everybody* deserves more careful attention than is really possible under these conditions."

Like with a great many of my encounters I've had with people along the military maze of this war, I am not entirely sure what the lieutenant wants out of this exchange. But I do get the feeling he doesn't always have this time and space to say his bit.

I take a stab at it. "Sure," I say. "Of course, you're right. It's important."

"They should all have this," he says sadly, but also with appreciation. "You don't have a big proper morgue up there in Chu Lai like we have here. But I already know from past experience that when a body has been prepped up there, it's been done right."

He's just a little bit more emotional than I would have figured a mortuary lieutenant to be. And I'm glad for it.

"I only saw the doc, the one who . . . you know . . . only saw him for a few seconds. I'm sure he was very precise. Not much bedside manner, though."

"Not much need for one, if you think about it."

"Good point. I keep trying not to think about it, though."

He nods. He looks both boyish and eternal. Like meeting your own grandfather when he's still young. There is a kind of hopeful expression that flits and flags across his face. That's rare enough around here, kind of miraculous in his job.

"It's a holy thing," he says, leaning in and making his case fervently. "Not necessarily religious-style holy. Way beyond that, as a matter of fact. I have yet to bring even one guy back once he's brought to me dead, but all the same I feel so sure, so sure, that my days here have as much impact on lives as anybody else's in the whole show."

Two groups of solemn, stout soldiers now march up to the plane, bearing coffins. To be honest, I'm glad for the company right now. The atmosphere's gotten so strange it would still be welcome if the two stiffs came and hopped aboard without anybody's help.

That was bad. *Stiffs.* That can never be right. What if somebody called my poor pal here a stiff? What would

I do? Grab the nearest gun and shoot him? Burst into tears? Both options feel about right.

"Right," Lt. Grafe says as he strides over to receive the first box personally by resting one hand on the lid while the six bearers carry on with carrying him on. "Once these two are settled in, that's your full complement of stiffs and you are free to be on your way to Tokyo."

I am shocked for about a second and a half. Grafe has got both hands placed lightly on top of the coffin when he utters the word, the *stiff* that sounds like a term of affection the way he uses it.

If I were dead, I would want Lt. Grafe overseeing my passage from wherever we are to wherever we go.

"Feetfirst, right?" I say, striding over to the men who clearly already know what they are doing. I need to be doing something. They are good men, and they let me.

The first coffin is aligned alongside Rudi. Then the next one eases in next to him. The boys all do the same unnecessary saluting to me as they turn away from their task, as they have turned away from it with the same grace three hundred forty-nine other times this month.

"Everything's settled here, yes?" I say, sidling along and inspecting the arrangement as if I am anything other than a joke here. I have to have something to do. Everybody has to have something to do.

The people here are so quiet. Quiet, and kind. I have experienced nothing like it since I arrived in Vietnam.

I feel a little better now that Rudi has peers to hang around with. I make a close inspection of the traveling angle of the three of them and then turn away, satisfied that nobody will be decomposing unnecessarily on my watch.

I pivot directly into the gaze of Lt. Grafe. The other guys have melted away like they were possibly never even here.

Maybe the two stiffs did deliver themselves. Maybe that's the way things happen in the Da Nang mortuary.

He's smiling at me. It makes me fidgety. He is so odd — decent, dedicated, unsettling. I wish he would just go now. Or alternatively, I wish he'd go and pull up that cargo-bay door and make this trip with me.

"Why are you telling me all this stuff?" I blurt. But I blurt it in a whisper so I don't know what you would call that.

If he is put off by my challenge I can see no sign of it.

Lt. Grafe shrugs and smiles shyly, as if he's a little bemused about it himself. But his words say otherwise.

"Because it's important," he says. "Because only part of war that is."

He needs to fight to hang on to his friendly smile during that last part, but he does fight, and he wins.

"I'm kind of a preacher, I guess," he says. "And my congregation is usually either too frantic or too deceased to hear me."

I nod, happy to understand this unusual, gentle soldier better.

"Well, I'm glad I was able to be here, unhurried and undead."

"And you heard me," he says, nodding vigorously before executing a sharp heel turn. He takes a couple steps, and salutes each coffin in turn. "Thank you, soldier," he says. "Thank you. And thank you."

He steps backward, pivots again, and comes to me.

I salute him crisply, more happy to do so than with almost all the other salutes so far. He waves off the salute, extends his hand and shakes. It is a surprisingly strong grip, capped with a second hand and some high-speed pumping.

"It's all yours now, friend," he says just before hopping off the plane. "A dignified departure. A gentle journey home."

"Gentle journey home," I echo as he waves and hot-steps across the airstrip toward his relentless roll call of departures to dignify.

It seems strange to call any aspect of this journey strange, what with the thorough strangeness of every other aspect, but I have to call the Da-Nang-to-Tokyo leg strange all the same.

First, I cannot stop thinking about the lieutenant's words. Or, not so much his words, maybe, as his . . . spirit? Life here, under these conditions, has taken on a different meaning, a different *status* from everything I ever knew from life back home. It's not that people — okay, soldiers — are so cold that they don't value lives anymore the way that regular citizens do —

Hold it. No. It is that. It is exactly that. How could it not be that?

We spend every day trying to slaughter as many as possible of the people we think need killing. Those people spend their days trying to slaughter our guys first, and anybody who doesn't believe they are doing pretty well at it should go and see Lt. Grafe for confirmation.

Life is less here, that's a fact. Most of us were not allowed to kill people before we got here and now we are *urged* to do it. Most of us did not start the average week with a group of buddies and coworkers knowing that some of them were sure to be too dead to start the following week with you. That is, if you were even there to start the next week.

It would be crazy if that reality did *not* alter the way people computed the whole life-death equation.

It matters. Of course it matters, and people feel the deaths of comrades deeply. But they do not feel them as much as they would feel them back home, back in their realer selves.

That's what made Lt. Grafe such a crosswind to everything else. With everybody else pulling away or numbing themselves or going out of focus or whatever works for self-preservation, that guy is making a point to make a connection — to make each life matter *more*, not less. And he's doing it at the point of life when every impulse says to let it go.

He cared about my boy as much as I did; he made me *feel* that Rudi mattered to him. I am ten thousand feet up and many miles out over the South China Sea before the impact of that hits me with a *bam*.

It gives me a searing ache to talk to Rudi about it right this minute. Did he notice? I hope he noticed. It's important. It's important for all of us.

I get up out of my seat, walk over to him, and I think I'm going to say something.

Then I don't. Can't. I freeze, seize, without warning, and I get flushed and hot.

It's the other two. I had talked to Rudi-in-the-box on the earlier leg and he was easy to talk to, easy as always. But now, I feel like I'm intruding. I feel like I'm doing something out of line.

I shuffle back to my seat and go back to staring out the window.

I'm sure he noticed, though. The few enough times anybody treated Rudi with any kind of respect, he would notice.

When we reach Tokyo, the other boys are transferred to another aircraft, headed for Alaska. I wouldn't have thought there were two soldiers from Alaska at all until this moment when I realize that two of them died in one single day. I feel good about the fact that they are keeping each other company through this whole awful trip. Then I feel bad thinking about how big a day it's going to be when they land in Anchorage.

But now, in the air again and on our way to California, it feels like me and Rudi again and that much is good.

He's an excellent listener.

"That was one irregular guy, that Lieutenant Grafe, huh? But it was very nice, the treatment you got. Good to remember that *somebody* cares, isn't it?"

I have relaxed enough, in our privacy, that I am actually leaning with both elbows on top of the coffin. Like I'm home already and ordering a butter-crunch ice cream at Brigham's. It is not the correct way to do this job, and I know that. It is the correct way with Rudi, in private. It is exactly the way he would want it, and I know that, too.

The three-man crew has been all but invisible to us the whole time. I suspect invisibility is a key skill with this particular duty.

"Somebody in the military, that is. Rudi, man, pretty soon we'll be seeing a bunch of people who care a whole lot. Your mom," I say, suddenly sucking in air as if I've startled myself. "My mom . . . Ah, jeez, Rude, Ivan's folks."

I shove myself up off the coffin and start pacing, because it doesn't feel like the casual ice-cream-parlor chat it was.

"I'm so scared, pal," I say, pacing faster. I walk away from him, use up the whole twenty feet of empty pace-space, pivot, come back to him. I do this mechanically, up and down and up like the fake rabbit they use to drive dogs nutty at the greyhound track at Wonderland.

Every time I reach Rudi's end, I touch the top of the box, pat it, rub it, just making contact.

"This is the hardest thing ever," I say. "How do I do this? I really wish Beck were here with us because then he'd for sure work it out. Or at least help me to slow it down and make it make sense.

"Which, right, makes no sense at all. Maybe it's better he's not here, because making this make sense makes no sense. It's so . . . unreal. Doesn't it feel like that, Rude? Anyway, thanks for listening. I feel better. Well, not really. But yeah. I could only ever go to Beck for real advice and stuff."

I am at the Rudi end of my circuit when I stop short, my hand flat on the top of his coffin.

"But now I have you," I say. "And it's good I can talk to you, before I get home. Because if I couldn't ever say it out loud, I think I would probably go all psychiatric discharge all over the place. Thanks. You're a good boy. Always were a good boy.

"I just had to talk to somebody who knows," I say, beginning my pacing again. But I get only four paces into it before my knees lock and I go statuesque. I reverse field and walk myself to Rudi's side again, put both my hands on the lid and lean low to him.

"Do you know?" I say, getting a shiver like there are small rats running up and down my spine. "What do you know, exactly, old pal?"

Just when the heavy, awful thing was lifting a bit, it comes back down heavier when I think about the very things I least want to think about.

"Aren't you supposed to suddenly have all the wisdom of the world when you die? So that all knowledge and understanding comes together and everything makes sense? Well, I think between here and home I'm going to need you to give me as much of that as you can manage, old buddy."

CHAPTER TEN

Rudi

I haven't laughed this much since high school. May not be saying too much since I just about stopped laughing from the time I left that place.

All the wisdom of the world.

Well, um, no.

Morris should accompany everybody home. He's the best guy, the *best* guy to do it because he's a gentleman and he doesn't make you feel like a jerk unless he absolutely has to, and whether or not he is smarter than you or tougher than you or cooler than you or richer than you or not dead like you or anything, he doesn't act like it. Whoever you are with Morris, he makes you feel less bad about it than anybody else ever would. Which is why he should be the guy for everybody's *gentle journey*.

And yeah, being handled by people with respect feels too nice to ever not notice. If I knew I could have gotten that treatment I would have gotten my brains shot out a lot of years ago.

Remember I used to cry all the time? Feels now like I have come all the way back to the me of then. Maybe that's what happens. It's like getting kept back times a zillion. Come this far and I'm *still* getting kept back. Hey, ha, maybe that means I'm in hell. Ha.

Still, maybe I got off easier than everybody else.

Probably more than maybe.

CHAPTER ELEVEN
Ivan

We are only a few miles now from reaching the base at Pleiku, and am I ever happy to be nearing home.

The attacks have gotten progressively worse all along the whole of Highway 19. Charlie, VC, NVA, who knows, maybe the Chinese and the Russians, too, are planted out there in the cover along the trail, because there is heavy, heavy firepower raining down on us. It's as if the entirety of the opposition forces has decided there is nothing more important at this juncture than stopping this very convoy from delivering anything at all to Pleiku.

But they have to. They have to deliver *me*.

Our adversaries are well on their way to achieving their goal as we make the final frantic dash along the decimated road. Trucks have been bombed out and eliminated ahead of our group and behind it with such regularity it feels like we have been not much more than gunnery practice for these boys. The gun trucks are vital and scrappy but right now their effect on the carnage is reduced to why-bother status.

And I am even more useless than that.

Our group has been reduced from ten vehicles to five, and by my count we have passed at least seven wrecks from the front group. It's all driving me fullbore demented as I sit on the floor and stare up at the smoky sky, because my beautiful rifle and I are meant for a different war altogether.

This is madness, what I am witnessing, and these guys are not giving a bit of concession to the obvious wipeout they are enduring. All three of these boys are still at it as if they have a chance to turn it around. Spent shell casings are flying back off of both gunners like a special kind of Vietnam hailstorm making a racket on the steel plating. The grenadier is spotting into the distance like a pro quarterback reading the defense and leading his wide receiver for the long bomb that's going to rescue the game in the final seconds. Then he rockets his grenade out there into the nothingness.

I have never felt so helpless and useless and humiliated and ashamed and spring-loaded as I do right now, trying to hold on for the last long miles 'til I can get back where I belong to fight the smart war I can fight and leave this chaotic sickness of a war to these guys who can handle it.

Bu-hooom, bu-hoom, bu-hooom, bu-hoom!

It is almost beyond the capacity of the senses to take in the enormity of what is happening now. I wouldn't have thought it possible, but the assault gets a whole lot worse as all the enemy firepower clustered in the run up to the base has coordinated to go for Armageddon right now.

I jump up to see what I can, and I see skies of flame ahead and behind us. There are now two cargo trucks and us in this group, and I wouldn't hold out a lot of hope that the other groups are faring any better.

Hope falls out of the equation entirely just a few seconds later, when we all go tumbling around as the driver slams the gun truck to a halt.

"Holy Moses," the grenadier says as we all bunch up at the front to survey the road before us.

The gun truck from the lead group has hit a land mine, is upturned and smoking from several places. There are human arms or legs or arms *and* legs trailing beside the armored box of the truck's platform. Like the one we are standing on right now. Could be two or three guys' limbs we're seeing, but I don't want to count because just the sight of them out there on their own, yards from the vehicle, is enough to make me comprehend what has happened.

The steel sidewalls built to protect them wound up chopping them up like fish at a market stall.

There appears to be enough space among all the wreckage that we could just about push through.

"Drive!" one of the gunners hollers down to the cab of our truck.

Nothing happens.

"Drive, drive, already!" yells the second gunner, with the same result.

I sling my canvas bag over my shoulder because I won't travel ten feet from this weapon, and I scramble over the side and down to the ground. I rush to the driver's door.

The ex-driver's door.

I can't even guess how many shots this silent partner of ours absorbed before finally giving out. There is too much blood and glass splashed all over him to count the wounds, but he sits upright, still gripping the wheel like all he needs is a quick rest and he'll be ready to roll again.

I throw open the door and shove the dead warrior across the seat to the shotgun side. "Sorry, man," I say sincerely as I toss my rifle in between us and put the truck into gear.

We tear through the demolition derby of our own smoldering trucks. I smash one of them on the way through hard enough to make it spin and skid away like a bumper car. I can hear the guys up top howling at my driving, but they'll just have to settle for the best I can manage.

This final stretch of road on the mountain approach to Pleiku is insanely treacherous. It seems like there is a sharp turn every twenty yards, with no margin for error on the downhill side, and I nearly tip off the edge taking the first two curves. The guys yell ever harder at me, but I just drive harder and hope they get used to us balancing on two wheels because in another minute they are going to have to go back into assault mode regardless.

It feels wrong, infuriating and embarrassing, to be losing like this, but losing we certainly are. We have all the machinery and the armor, the firepower and personnel. The base right up there with all those resources. And still we get smacked around, because the enemy knows better.

It's *their* home field, after all, and they fight like holding on to it has more meaning than a thousand foreign armies could ever understand. They are surely right about that, as very few American GIs I've met have any notion at all what their own mission is about, let alone appreciating — or caring to appreciate — what the other side is thinking. I look over to my copilot, whose scalp wounds are raining a shiny blood mask over his eyes. He doesn't want to know.

The truth is, if anybody asked me to explain what it is we are doing here, I'd have trouble putting it into words. It's just possible I understand Charlie's position better than ours, because I have put myself into those slippers of his and imagined how viciously I'd go for his throat, and his buddy's and his mother's and his dog's, if they came to *my* country looking to shoot up the place.

There is that, and the fact that these boys all seem to know every rut and shrub and hollow of their country to a level I don't even know my own hometown. It almost seems too easy for them at times like this, and I am *raging* right now to be sniping again, doing the business of bringing the maximum of death to these merciless creatures. One, by one, by one, by one, by one. The way it should be.

If I get there. Because presently they appear to have the run of the mountain, roaming free and invisible.

As I careen around the next turn, I feel the presence of Vietcong guerrillas all along the down slope to our right. And suddenly they are up in the hillside to our left, too, right under the chins of the men stationed at Pleiku.

I overcompensate on the turn, fearing I might topple right over the edge this time. The two left wheels drop into a rut off the side of the road. The former driver comes tumbling over onto me, his forehead conking my right eyebrow in a sharp head butt. I grab his face with my right hand and I throw him with enough force to slam him into the far door. Then I just manage to yank the wheel at the correct angle to remount the road without tipping us over in the process.

"Sorry again, pal," I say, casting a glance at his sad self, crumpled and unappreciated and more in the foot well than on the seat. All wrong for a hero's ending, but exactly how it looks here in real life.

It is when I look away from him and straight ahead that it finally comes.

The crackle-storm of small- and medium-caliber-arms fire erupts all at once, filling the air. I don't even have the chance to react before my head snaps back and I feel the fire inside my face. A bullet has hit me smack in my right cheekbone, and the burning of the flesh quickly becomes nothing compared to the shell-shatter of bone inside.

The light goes right out of that eye. I floor the accelerator and drive straight into the attack out of a simple lack of any other ideas. I keep the one eye open and the head as low as I dare and plow through a bullet barrage that sounds like a whole company of machine gunners is honoring us with all their attention. For their part, the guys upstairs sound like they have all bunched up at the front rail, ignoring the crossfire from up and down the mountain to pour everything they've got into the troops straight ahead of us.

Thoughts of my dad flood my head as I recognize the Little Bighorn nature of the moment.

The final unaccounted-for truck of the forward group is run off the road and banked at a forty-five-degree angle facing a boulder as big as itself. There are ten or so VC machine gunners lying flat in the grass in front of the truck and at least a couple of snipers firing at us from behind the boulder. They are wasting an awful lot of ammunition right now trying to kill the crew of this one gun truck. But they must figure it's more than compensated for by the haul they are taking at the same time.

Like a stream of upright, black-pajama-wearing

army ants, VC fighters are running a seemingly infinite supply line from the back of that truck, that *American* truck, right across the road, and down the steep slope to anonymity on the other side. The truck was rigged out with ammo resupply for the base, which explains why they surgically isolated it from the pack and took it down with small arms and no bombs.

They like to kill us and blow all our operations to oblivion.

But they *love* to kill us and then take our munitions off us in the bargain.

And kill us with our own stuff.

The air is thick with smoke and bullets as both sides give it everything. I squint with my good eye just at steering-wheel level and stick to the road. One of our grenades explodes on the other side of the boulder and parts of at least one sniper fly up and splat down on the rock and the fighters in front of it. The gunners upstairs are rightly isolating the shooters as the thieving ants hightail it across the road, weighed down with all our gear.

Then my grenadier turns their way as we come within about thirty yards of the scene. He rockets a grenade right at the ground, at the point where the road meets the VC escape route down the hill.

Puwhaaam!

The outside section of the road bursts into the air with the explosion, then several smaller explosions as the haul of ammo goes up, along with rocks and earth and probably four dead and decimated Vietcong unfortunates. Rocks and bloody pieces of dead come down on what remains of the windshield; at the same moment I slam five tons of thundering gun truck into three slow-footed foot soldiers who are barely tall enough to see me over the hood before I get them.

The truck hardly registers the slamming of the three bodies until they are crushed underneath and some of the ordnance explodes beneath our steel-plated under-carriage. We do a small bump, a hop, a burp, really, as we barrel on over the bodies and past the firefight and make the next bend toward Pleiku.

They were so small. Everybody knows that, I know. But there they were. So small. And then there they weren't. With me crouching so low they probably thought they were getting run down by a haunted, driverless truck. If they got to think anything at all.

There is a very welcome quiet when we make that turn, as the ambush seems to have been the finale of the long siege.

I am conscious of attempting to control a lot of competing processes within myself right now. I am breathing deeply to keep from panting with the rush of adrenaline and fear and rage and defeat and the vengeance of killing enemies of any size who needed killing and invited killing. I am trying to relax, to shift out of my hyper-adrenaline state enough to maybe slow the blood that is pulsing out of my face with the rhythm of a pump working to empty a flooded boat. I am trying to balance that impulse with the need to keep enough adrenaline going to be able to drive. The bandage on my forehead has certainly done all it can up there, so I tear it off now, and more or less stuff it into the hole of my cheek to stanch the bleeding there. I feel the bone fragments behind the stuffing shift and crunch with the pressure.

". . . have to listen! Are you listening to me?!"

I become aware that I'm being yelled at when the voice is boosted by a crazed hammering on the roof right over my head. I lean left into what is less a window than a small rectangular earhole cut into the steel plate where a window would otherwise be.

"What?" I yell back.

"Stop, man. You gotta stop. Right now. We gotta go back!"

For good or bad — and almost certainly it would

have to be bad — that catches my attention and I brake hard, right there in the middle of the road.

I pause for just a few seconds to sniff the air for trouble, but the quiet smells real. I open the door and step out onto the road.

It's the grenadier. He's been hammering my roof with somebody's helmet and now he is standing tall up there with a handgun in one hand and his rocket launcher in the other.

"Are you alone up there?" I ask.

"Didn't you have a whole complete face last time I saw it?"

"Don't answer a question with a question."

"Don't ask stupid questions, then. Of course I'm alone up here. The miracle is that there's even one of us left. How bad is that wound? Looks nasty. You gonna be all right? Can you drive?"

The slug in my facial framework feels like, in fact, a slug. Feels like a thing that is both metal and alive, piercing and swelling as it seems to navigate its way deeper into my skull. My right eyeball feels like somebody's got it in his fist and is squeezing it like one of those hand exercisers.

"I am going to be all right and I can drive. What is it?"

"We have to go back. The truck, the driver. Man's alive."

"You know that?"

"I saw him. As we were pulling away. I looked; he was in the cab, at the wheel, faking it. He signaled to me. Waved. Should have seen. We can't leave him. I waved back. We gotta get him. Can't leave him to those people. If they find him out . . . We just can't. Don't know who else is gonna be coming up the road, if anybody. We gotta do it."

"That's right," I say. "We do. Any spare automatic weapons up there?"

He disappears for a couple of seconds and returns to chuck his sidearm down to me.

Depth perception is different now, I realize as the weapon practically clobbers me. I thought I had it clean, but it grazes my arm and thumps my shoulder on its way down. I pick it up and as soon as I look again he's tossed me a small metal lockbox with ammunition.

"There's a new cartridge in the gun. You got a few more full clips in the box," he says. "Very unlikely you'll get the chance to use them up, but hey, we can hope, right?"

"Right," I say, throwing the ammo box onto the seat.

I am leaning into the cab once more when he calls me back.

"Hey!" he barks. "You got a name?"

I smile at him, thinking he's really rushing things, since we just met and all.

"No, I don't," I say, and jump back into the truck.

"DelValle," he calls as I'm about to shut the door behind me. "Nice to know you."

The slam of the door rocks my hurting head and I try to think why that name rings, and how it lifts me briefly to better things.

But the grinding of the gears and the straining of the truck's engine drag me right back down to the horror of this. I spin the wheel all the way right to start the arc that starts the dash back into the pit of the impossible, just down that hill.

As we are rumbling down I glance right at my still crumpled, collapsed associate and think — because I am trying to think about anything other than the zero odds we are galloping into — that nobody rides for free in the United States Army in wartime.

Death is no excuse.

I lean way over and grab a fistful of the bloody shoulder of his shirt, and with a mighty heave I haul him over to my side. Then, with a second effort, I pull him up onto my lap. I maneuver him into his old driver's seat while I shimmy partway over to the shotgun side. I am driving, awkwardly, from this off-center angle, but as far as my one working left eye is concerned, the view looks as straight on as it should. I am leaning hard with my left shoulder into the guy to keep him roughly in place as a dummy driver when we round that critical bend in the other direction. The wind slapping us through the glassless windshield frame is just about enough to revive me, if not my partner, and I feel as ready as I can be for this.

The sound of a relentless firefight persists as if they never stopped shooting at our memory.

But as we roar down, guns a' blazin', we realize that they are firing downhill, at the intrepid second gun truck and the sole cargo vehicle to have persevered this far. The VC are caught completely off guard by our return — and why wouldn't they be?

We drive straight and crazy toward the crippled cargo truck with the faking-dead driver at the wheel. DelValle launches one grenade at the nest of gunners firing downhill and it explodes ten feet behind them, blasting two of them toward heaven along with a dense cloud of earth and rock. Several others are blown tumbling sideways with the impact, and when they stop rolling they reset flat on the ground and point our way.

DelValle opens fire on them with the machine gun and draws their fire in return. I grip the wheel with my right hand and try to aim the automatic pistol with my left, but it's too awkward to aim this way, so I shift back to behind the steering wheel, with my bloody buddy now jammed tight right in front of me.

We're swooping down on their position as I join DelValle in pouring automatic gunfire down on top of these guys. The body in front of me jerks and judders and reverberates with the dozen and more and then more rounds pounding and penetrating this unknown soldier who has not yet stopped giving for his country. I feel a piercing pain in my neck and my collar bone as the body is annihilated, thrown harder and harder up against me with the force. But all the while I keep firing rounds straight into the spot where the bullets are coming from until the clip is empty.

From downhill, the other gun truck's remaining two gunners are also firing on them, and the VC are caught frazzled for the first time I've ever seen. I seize the moment, jumping the truck off the side of the road and cruising right down alongside the looted vehicle.

Its driver sits straight up in his seat and clambers

over to the opposite side and out the window. He falls awkwardly with a thud to the ground between our vehicles, while the sound of gunfire continues to crackle and whistle in the air all around us. In a few seconds that feel like a week, the soldier appears on the other side of my truck, pulls open the door, and flops himself onto the seat. I tear away immediately but he manages to get upright and just about pull the door shut with his one hand that does not look as if it's been run through an industrial sausage maker.

He says nothing as I execute a reasonable doughnut maneuver in circling all the way around his truck on my way back to the road. My human shield flops his pulpy self back over into the lap of our new guest, who receives him silently and graciously.

Around the other side of the truck we are hit again with a smattering of bullets.

But they are from our guys.

The gun truck's last fighter and one guy with a machine gun on top of the cargo truck have continued to hold out against the machine-gun nest. They abruptly hold fire on seeing us roar into their view and their line of fire, and we cut back toward the road and right over the spines of unblinking and unaware Vietcong shooters. I feel the bumps in sequence this time, as one and two and three bodies crush under my wheels before they can shoot one single more anybody.

I don't stop to listen to the reassuring silence behind me. I continue on my intended route, up the bank and onto the road to Pleiku with the people who need to be dead dead on the ground behind me. Lying down and flat like that, who could tell how big or small they were, if that even mattered. All the same, lying down and trying to kill us. All the same.

I hear the other two vehicles, the only other two remaining of the entire convoy, it turns out, rev right up close behind me as we see our mission through to the end together, in a formation of sorts.

PART
TWO

Have I stopped talking at all?" I ask Rudi as our final flight touches down. I know the answer, I know I have not been able to stop because every mile closer to home makes me more anxious and I don't know what to do but keep talking, talking to Rudi. I count on him being too polite to tell me to shut up.

I feel it bubbling up in my stomach now, the nerves that are all about the horrors of home. I was exactly this scared when I first arrived *in* Vietnam, and it probably stands as a perfect summary of the whole experience that I am bringing it all the way home with me. Perfect, and perfectly wrong.

I talked from Honolulu to Norton Air Force Base in California. I talked from Norton all the way to Dover Air Force Base in Delaware, which is where we are finally touching down for good.

"Thanks, Rudi, man," I say as I hear the preparations outside for receiving us, processing us, and sending us on a train ride to Boston. My voice sounds hoarse and strange, not like me at all, but that would be expected, I suppose. I have talked out my concerns over my next posting, and about what kind of reception active military personnel could expect coming back from the war, and I talked about our mothers, Rudi's and mine, and I believe it was right about there that my voice kind of snapped.

What I did not talk about was Ivan. Or Beck. I didn't even venture back into stories from when we were kids, even though I thought about it and badly wanted to. Minefields there, I fear. World of hurt there.

It sounds like more than just overuse. It sounds changed, and I am not comfortable with the change. It freaks me out and makes me, finally, want to just be quiet.

"Is that the wisdom-of-the-dead thing?" I say, laughing with ol' Rudi as the cargo door is opening and the world prepares to intervene in our last-ever time alone together. "You couldn't tell me to shut up, so you just went and zapped my power of speech?"

I am raspy-laughing when I turn to the open door to find an Army officer standing in the light and smiling generously at me.

I may have slightly mistimed my last private moment with Rudi.

"Nothing to be embarrassed about, sailor," he says, offering me his hand to shake. "I know as well as anyone just how chatty these comrades can be when they get you alone."

I take his hand as I hop down out of the plane. Then we step aside and let the detail of six Air Force personnel board and take our comrade down.

Dignified transfer is what they pride themselves on here, and that is what we experience. I feel like I am a war widow or something with the careful and respectful way I'm treated. The officer, Captain Morrison, has to make sure that identification, transfer orders, and assorted papers are all in order before he can send us on. But when I realize his duties are diverging from the path the airmen are taking my friend, I go into a small fret-fit over not being able to go both directions. Captain Morrison needs me, over at his office. But Rudi needs me, over at the transfer depot at the far end of the hangar building.

And so, I freeze right there in the middle of the sprawling and busy facility, helping nobody, accomplishing nothing.

I am overcome right now with indecision, and weakness, and loss and fear and a bottomless sadness, and I am just about to pick the worst setting any member of the armed forces has ever picked to fall completely to pieces. I want to go with Rudi. But I see him being taken away and I am physically unable to respond in any way.

I feel like I'm abandoning him.

"Yes, indeed," Captain Morrison says in my ear, "this is the largest mortuary facility in the entire United States Armed Services. It can be a bit overwhelming, I know. Have you slept, son?" he says, with an arm so skillfully around my shoulders I hardly know he's moving me until I am there, in his office. "Since you left Vietnam? What was that, three, four days?"

All I can manage is to shake my head, no, even though I could be answering one of those questions by accident and not the other.

"Eaten?"

When I try to smile at him and then look over my shoulder and out his office window toward Rudi's absence, he draws his own conclusions. He gets on the phone and rattles off some quick orders while plowing through the paperwork. Within minutes somebody in cook's whites is placing a hot roast-beef sandwich, fries, potato salad, and dill pickle wedges on the desk in front of me. There is a drink I believe to be ice tea. A Hershey's chocolate bar.

I look across the table at the captain while he barrels through all the formalities.

"This is a lot of food, sir," I say.

He stops what he's doing, rests his chin on his entwined fingers.

"You know, there are lots of crazy regulations in this part of personnel management. Some of them so crazy you might be tempted to think somebody like me just made them up himself. One of those is, we do not release precious cargo such as our friend out there to the care of men suffering from starvational dementia. And we also clean our plates, because waste is a sin. So, in order for me to put you two servicemen onto that train, at least one of you has got to eat that. It probably should be you."

I am chewing roast beef before he has even picked his pen back up.

I feel unfeasibly better as the captain walks me across the facility floor to be reunited with the other member of my party. I still have the apprehension of what awaits in Boston, but I don't feel anything like the helplessness that was overtaking me pre-meal.

"I appreciate it, sir," I say.

"Magic beef they serve here, isn't it?"

"Yes, sir, it is that."

"Try and get some sleep on the ride up, please?" he says. "You may well find you need whatever resources you can store up."

"I'm thinking listening to you in this instance is preferable to listening to myself right now so, yes, sir, I will sleep, sir."

"Good," he says as we reach the truck that will take us to the train station. There are three men in the front seat so I know I'm back in the bed with Rudi. I circle around to get in and see that now, we are really there.

The coffin is draped. The United States flag is blanketing our fallen Marine, in the proper fashion with the blue over his face. He's not hiding what he is now, not just a crate of cargo or a Rudi-in-the-box.

"It is a hard business, this," Captain Morrison says, giving my back a firm pat as if I might not make it up there into the truck on my own. "And you are doing something important beyond words, for his family as well as ours. Thank you."

"Thank you," I repeat in my raspy, foreign voice.

It's really it now. We won't be waking up.

CHAPTER THIRTEEN

Ivan

This was not supposed to be my war.

It was supposed to be me and my rifle, alone, stalking the enemy, dependent on no one. Bringing the maximum of death to the minimum of people.

I should never have left the highlands.

And for *what*? There's no such thing as a reunion.

"I'm sorry, lieutenant," says the soldier who arrives at the foot of my bed. "I checked on that and I'm afraid he didn't survive."

"Didn't survive," I repeat from behind my faceful of bandages.

"No, sir."

I nod. He leaves.

I wonder if anything survives Vietnam.

CHAPTER FOURTEEN
Beck

I wonder what on earth I am doing here now.

It's the same as before Chu Lai. I am flight engineer on an AC-47 gunship, a "Spooky." We still fly close-support missions for ground troops when they radio in for help. We still swoop in, flying low in great big left-handed loops, firing down on the area until our boys can either advance or retreat safely due to our eliminating trouble for them. Just the same as before Chu Lai.

Except that nothing is the same as before Chu Lai.

I returned to Da Nang to be reunited with my refurbished Spooky and then we flew it immediately back to Phu Cat. All through that trip I wondered to myself what I was going to do with the rest of my tour. Less than two months left, making me that precious creature we all wanted to be — the "two-digit midget" who has under a hundred days left in-country. I always figured no matter how bad things got here I would be able to persevere once I got to this stage.

That certainty did not accompany me back from Chu Lai.

And now we are back up in the air and cruising to another hot spot because somebody on the ground has called for close air support and Captain Gilroy was only too happy to tell me not to bother settling in because I was going right back up.

I hate Captain Gilroy.

I hate this war and I hate this plane and I hate my job and I hate this Air Force and the armed services and all armed services, and I may have been able to patch over all those small obstacles to doing my duty before Chu Lai but there is serious doubt as to whether I can do it now.

Everything on board is functioning factory fresh on the tuned-up plane, so my jobs are presently minimal and I slip to a small observational window as we reach our designated area. I can just see the firefight below when we start banking into the elliptical pattern from which we will pummel our enemy.

All to protect our boys.

My ears start ringing as the heavy guns of the Spooky erupt and the air fills with our firepower.

It sounds so much louder than I remember it. It's as if there is a gunfight going on inside the plane with us. I cover my ears and watch the battle on the ground.

And I wonder who the fighters down there might be.

Before Chu Lai, when the captain forced me to man one of the guns, I could believe that there was a chance I was directly defending my old pal Rudi from harm, and that got me through my reservations about killing, about war, about pointless aggression. Because there *was* a point.

If I thought I might be protecting Rudi, then I could shoot somebody to do that, no doubt about it. But Rudi's not down there; he's dead.

If I thought I might be protecting Morris, snaking up-country on some tiny tributary surrounded by banks of bloodless VC killers, then I could do that. But Morris isn't down there anymore, either; he's rotated back home.

And if I thought Ivan was down there now?

What if I thought Ivan was down there now?

"Beck!" Captain Gilroy screams as I continue to watch the action unfold with my hands insufficiently covering my ears. "Beck!"

What *am* I doing here?

"Beck!"

My, how I hate that guy.

CHAPTER FIFTEEN

Morris

Rudi and I have our own carriage on the train. It is easily the most royal treatment either of us has ever had. But it's coming to an end now as we make the approach into South Station.

I slept probably an hour in total, which is probably less than Captain Morrison had in mind, but I am feeling sharpish. It is the pounding of my heart, not the nap, that is the more likely cause of my readiness. Not that I feel *ready*. I don't believe I am ready at all.

We come to a stop. From outside, somebody pulls the door open and I step to the edge of the carriage to see what I can see, must see.

I'm a bit stunned to see The Captain, Ivan's dad, saluting me from the platform, and behind him an honor guard of Marines.

"Oh," I gasp, as unmilitary a sound as any military escort has likely ever made. But I manage to return his salute before stumbling down the steps.

"How are you, Morris?" The Captain says, shaking my hand and patting my other shoulder at the same time.

"Um, thank you, sir," I say. "Fine, I mean. I mean, as fine as . . . I suppose . . . Well, you know . . . I suppose."

"I know," he says with an understanding nod.

I didn't give much thought to who was going to meet the train. I guess I assumed Rudi's mom, and mine. Somebody from the Marines, certainly, but . . .

Is my head ever going to stop spinning?

The honor guard mounts the carriage and gets to the business of dignified transport.

"You do look lost, Morris, I must say," says The Captain.

Ivan's dad, The Captain.

"Yes, sir," I say.

The two of us stand at attention, saluting, as Rudi's flag-draped coffin comes down and passes by on the way to the hearse that has been brought right up into the station, twenty yards from the train. Once he is loaded inside and the back is shut on him, we relax. So to speak.

I watch as the hearse pulls very slowly away from

us, and I feel my voice cracking without my having to attempt a word.

The Captain takes a firm grip of my upper arm and leads me in the opposite direction. But I still keep looking back at the hearse.

We are separated now. There he goes, no longer mine.

I am watching my old world passing by my window as The Captain talks to me from the driver's seat.

"I took the liberty of liaising with the military authorities and the funeral home to get things together as simply and smoothly as possible," he says. "I know this is hard enough already for everyone."

"Thank you, sir," I say without looking at him.

"That's why you were stuck with me to greet you."

"I didn't feel stuck at all, sir."

"His mom couldn't do it. She was intending to, but . . ."

"I understand."

I am aware of this getting more and more awkward despite the fact that this is a good man making every effort to do right by everyone. That could even be making the situation worse, but still, it's not his fault and he deserves better.

He deserves a whole lot better.

"So, naturally, your mom thought she should stay with her."

"Of course."

"It's been an unbearably hard time for everyone here. As, of course, it has been for you boys over there. Possibly even more so."

"I can't imagine," I say, "that anything could be harder than it is for the parents."

"You are a thoughtful boy, Morris. I have been trying to talk to Ivan since we heard, but have not been able to contact him yet. Have you seen him, since? Do you know how he's doing? I worry very much, since he and Rudi were so —"

"No, sir. I did see him not long before. But . . . I'm sure you understand things got completely out of control after that."

"Of course," he says. "Of course I understand. . . ." He is a great man, The Captain. He is juggling everything for everybody right now. He is military and he is friend, he is liaison and he is driver. He is mourner and he is stand-in, for a couple of women who don't have husbands to lean on. For sons who don't have fathers.

He is all that, and he is heroic.

And he is still more.

"I just," he says with a gaping pause right there, "would like to know that he's all right. If I could just hear him or see him, or touch his big blocky head with my own hands and know that he is all right . . . that would be good. That would be good."

"That would be good," I say.

I don't pretend I can give him the reassurance I cannot give him. We drive on through the streets and neighborhoods in silence until we come to the streets that join us all together, that join our houses with our school and our history and with the funeral home.

"Are you ready?" he says as we pull up in front of his house and all of our people.

Now I look at him.

"No," I say.

The Captain nods at me, pulls away from the curb, and in a few minutes he is depositing me at another curb, in front of my own house.

"No," he insists as I step out of the car. "Now, Morris, we all appreciate how grueling this journey has been for you. You have done as much as you can for now. You simply must go to your bed before you collapse from exhaustion, which nobody wants to see. And that is a direct order, which I will explain to everyone. Is that clear?"

This is an awfully good man. Which makes it hurt all the worse.

"Thank you, sir."

"No," he says softly, "thank *you*."

CHAPTER SIXTEEN

Ivan

DelValle. DelValle the grenadier didn't make it.

Evelyn DelValle. That was it, what rang the bells, what gave me the one moment of unidentifiable *nice* in the middle of all that brutality.

Boy, did we love her. Boy, was she worth fighting for. Maybe together we could have added up to one guy worthy. One guy good enough for Evelyn DelValle could surely fight the world in a war and win.

Worth fighting for, for sure.

But we wouldn't fight each other. Not for anything.

CHAPTER SEVENTEEN
Morris

I barely remember going to bed.

"Morris?" I hear from somewhere in the clouds. "Morris? I'm sorry."

I know. Everybody is sorry. Everybody knows everybody is sorry so we don't have to say it anymore.

"I'm sorry, son, but you have to wake up now. It's time. I've left it as long as I dare."

I roll over, blink a hundred times, and take in the vision of my beautiful, sad ma standing, hands folded, dressed in black.

"Hiya, Ma," I say, extending both my hands to her.

"Hiya," she says, taking them. She nods her get-along-now nod of gentle persuasion.

"Already?" I ask.

"I'm afraid so."

"It's all going so fast now. After it went so slow for so long."

"I know," she says. "She wanted it done this way. Mr. Bucyk has organized with the Marines people every step of the way. There's a brief service at the church this morning. Then the cemetery with the military thing. . . ."

The military thing. The military *thing*.

"Then, all done and dusted," I say, sneering like I would have just two or three years ago when she'd be right where she is now, trying to roust me for school.

She looks down at the floor, giving me a second for composure while never letting go of my hands. Then she looks up.

"Sorry, Ma," I say.

She gives the hands a squeeze before letting go.

"No need for that," she says. "Just get ready now. We're almost late."

Banana, orange juice, English muffin with grape jelly constitute the fuel that powers me out of the house.

Ma and I walk the few blocks to the church, me in my Navy uniform, her in her mourning one. I am happy to think about other things than where we are going as we stroll through the old neighborhood on a cool sunny morning. What I think immediately is that the place seems smaller again, smaller even than when I came back last time. And the people we pass, some distantly familiar and some not at all, look likewise smaller than the people I knew when I knew this place.

The uniform draws attention. It draws no comment, however, probably due to the dignified woman in black on my arm. I am aware how the war is playing out at home, and that almost nobody is neutral on it. I feel like everybody would like to shout something if they could, and I wish they could so I could know better where I stand.

But as I scan the faces I don't know if I do want to know.

There are so many memories attached to these granite steps attached to this redbrick church. They bombard me as the two of us walk gently up to the entrance: first Communion, first confession, small parts in earnest Christmas plays, confirmation . . . and boredom, the feeling of being trapped Sunday after Sunday made bearable by having three or two or even just one other guy to laugh with hysterically for no other reason than we must not, must not laugh.

Even just the one guy.

Rudi *never* missed Mass. He liked gatherings of people.

"It's open," I say to Ma as the two of us walk up the aisle, nearly late and certainly last, like a deeply strange wedding couple.

"Yes," she says calmly, knowingly.

Cripes, I hadn't even thought about this. I have been with Rudi's dead body all along, and I got used to a task that most people will never have to get used to, but I am freaking now over the open casket and the task we in this church have been used to forever.

Aw, cripes.

We split the aisle and the small gathering of family members and fancy-dressed Marines, and we stop a few feet short of the coffin, then Ma goes up to kneel before it and say the good good-bye she has practiced in this old building all those other times, and I am sure it is comforting to Rudi but now she is done, neat and tidy, and I don't know if I can do any of that: neat, tidy, or comforting.

She brushes me lightly on her way past, and I am officially up.

Last time I saw him?

Good Lord, no.

I'm bawling like a fool before I hit my knees and I haven't even seen his face yet. I was wailing out of control last time, too, that last time, that last time I saw

Rudi's sweet, stupid face, and I was pushing and pushing on his chest. When I look up now I'm sort of doing it again because I have both my hands out and resting on the double breast of his sharp Marine jacket with the polished buttons, but there is exactly the same absence underneath my sweaty palms now as there was then.

I am trying my guts out not to do the slobbering blubbering I did on that trail that time, but I do hear the cavernous old church echoing all around with my sniffles and snuffles as I try to hold things together like the hardened soldier I am supposed to be after all.

I see his face, though, and Lord, look at it. It is small and it is innocent and simple as the day I met him, and while I am as happy as I could be to think that we will give back to the earth today the good and fine Rudi boy that we found in the first place and not that hard and demented one we had messed up so bad there at the end, I have to fight the howl I feel rising when I see that we are sending the good boy off with the big hole right there in his puttied and powdered temple.

The hardest thing, easily. The hardest thing I have ever done is this thing I am doing, and it is mostly not-doing that I am doing. I want to bellow and roar to the point where my voice will roll around these stone walls repeating *Rudi* for the rest of time.

They did what they could. But the spot with the sniper's mark looks like a hole in a tire tube blown out and patched in desperation.

The bells ring. The great bells of the church tower ring and resonate, singing out that the appointed hour is here. It's twelve o'clock. The time has come, and my hope of walking back down that aisle without a scene is no hope at all.

I cannot stop.

Sorry, man.

I give Rudi one last two-handed chest thump, then use the bells like close air support as I make my way, head down, back to the pew.

CHAPTER EIGHTEEN

Rudi

Embarrass me, why dontcha.

I could always do that pretty good myself, though, right?

We are supposed to be done with all that *sorry* stuff, remember? So, no more, okay? Okay? Okay.

Remember Peters Hill? Wetting my pants over the induction notice? Something to cry about? Ha. Now that's something to cry about. You all hugged me anyway, wet pants and all.

Remember? Remember that?

We were one. We really were one.

Remember?

Do. Remember.

CHAPTER NINETEEN

Beck

I have to sleep. I need sleep.

It's past eleven, and I have to sleep.

I can't go back to my bunk until this stops. I will stay in this toilet until it stops because otherwise they will think I am losing it and I won't have that. I will hold it together because I can. Because I won't be one of them. I have the tools; I will not break.

I cannot stop the crying. I don't know why. I have to, though, or I'll just be another one of them, another broken, pathetic casualty, and I will not be that.

I will sleep right where I am if need be. I am better than this, I am stronger than this. I am smarter than this. I should be able to figure it out, and I should be able to stop it.

I cannot stop.

I am so sorry.

Peters Hill. Still can't believe he peed his pants. Doofus.

Magnificent doofus.

I jam my fist right into my mouth when one final great howl of horror comes up to get it all out of me, finally.

It will stop. It will, it is, it will. And I will sleep.

He peed his pants. Ha. Remember.

CHAPTER TWENTY

Ivan

You have one eye, moron.

You only have one left.

You cannot rub it like that and expect it to survive. Like you are grinding flour.

Go to sleep. That's an order. Eleven p.m. Lights out. You want to get better? Huh? Do you? Do you want to get better?

I'm so sorry.

This has to stop. There are other patients. There are *personnel* about. Don't want this on your chart. Do not want this on your chart. Stop it. Shut up, grow up, toughen up.

I am so sorry.

Get it out, then. Get it out. Be done, be gone, be away, now.

What else? Huh? Wet the bed yet?

Ha.

Peters Hill. Should we smile? Would that be terrible?
Is any smile now terrible?

Crazy chicken, wetting his pants. Ha.

Ah.

We were one, we were.

Rudi

Bunch of Rudi-Judies, one and all.

That's what I say.

Rudi-Judy, Rudi-Judy, Rudi-Judy.

Now I'll never get any rest, watching out for you guys.

CHAPTER TWENTY-TWO

Morris

The turnout is sickeningly small.

What is wrong with the people here?

I am standing on the side of the open grave, where friends and family are all lined up, and you could hardly call it a crowd. I don't see anybody from school. I am positioned at the corner of the grave closest to the street, where I can see every person here, and if we wanted to follow up the service with a memorial softball game we wouldn't be able to field two full teams. All of our parents are here, as if they were part of the deal when the four of us pledged to stay together and they are the ones who are actually seeing it through.

What if they knew, though?

Holy cow, what if they knew? Where would we be?

There are a few other mourners I can't quite place as Rudi's relatives or as neighbors or just those freaks who go to funerals, but that is it.

His mother wanted it quick, though, for her own reasons, so that didn't help bring a crowd.

Or didn't help expose the lack of one.

Short and sweet was what she wanted. She got one of them.

As the priest says his few more words and the end is very, very nigh, I focus on who *is* here, who *does* care.

The Marines. There is a Marine honor guard at the far side of the grave, and they look, I have to say, magnificent. They are sharp and solemn and attentive, and there are *eight* of them, and they look like they could field a whole team by themselves.

Rudi would be ecstatic. And he earned it.

I am not listening to the priest, I confess. I am listening to the breeze and to myself and looking and looking and looking at faces, and so I only know what is happening when it happens and the priest stops talking and the commander of the guard barks in hushed barks and the six Rudi-bearers go to the coffin and line up for the end. Four of them take the flag by its corners and step sideways with it. With precise, practiced movements they fold the stars and stripes, fold again and again until it is a beautiful puffed triangular pillow. The commander takes the flag and walks up to Rudi's mom.

He goes down on one knee in the grass.

The commander makes a speech from his kneeling position as he hands Rudi's mom the flag.

"I offer my apologies to you, ma'am, on behalf of the United States Marine Corps, for the supreme sacrifice you have had to make for your country . . ."

It gets very hard to hear words now.

". . . and the nation's gratitude for the courage and heroism of your son in giving up his life for a duty . . ."

The words are water now. Water and wind until they are nothing and the commander stands, marches back to his spot, and barks a bark that sets the bearers in motion. They collect their ends of the three satin ropes running under Rudi's coffin and they lift him up. As they walk toward the fresh grave, three on each side, the final member of the honor guard raises his bugle as the others lower the fallen soldier into the ground.

Taps plays clearly through the air, through the people, through the trees that surround the pretty cemetery that lies here in the shadow of Peters Hill.

I listen as it plays out, lovely, perfect. I look up to that spot on the hill as it does, not at the hole in the ground, because now we are done with crying, and this is a lot better. It is.

I still can't believe you peed your pants, man. Right there.

I am pointing right at the spot, and I hope nobody is upset at the pointing and the smile I cannot do anything about.

I have decided to walk by myself to the reception after the burial and everyone has decided to allow me that. I enjoy solitude more and more these days, partly as a result of military life, where you are almost never alone. It's also, at least right now it is, a result of my being in this town, walking these streets, without the team I had always walked them with before.

It was a very isolated feeling there at Rudi's funeral. Even he had his team there, the Marines.

My team is blown up, and I don't know what parts of it can ever be reunited.

And to top it all off, the reception is being hosted by Ivan's parents.

I mean, nobody would have thought Rudi's mom would be capable of hosting anything, but this feels like the final joke on Rudi, in a life that was full of jokes on him.

As I walk up the stairs to Ivan's front porch, I am

already trying to figure out my exit strategy before conversations get too uncomfortable.

My ma, because she is a good and attentive ma, sweeps right over to me as I walk in the door.

"I don't think I can do this for very long, Ma," I say.

"I understand," she whispers back while at the same time maneuvering me right into harm's way. "Just do as much as you can while you're here. It means a lot to have you here."

"I know," I sigh.

"I'm very proud of you," she says as she shoves me right up to face Rudi's mom.

"Well, it's over now," she says as we embrace for a few awkward seconds. She is seated at the Bucyks' dining room table and I have to bend down to meet her. I straighten back up to see a cup of tea, a scone, and a folded flag on the table before her.

"You visited him, didn't you?"

"Yes, ma'am, I did."

"How did he seem? I mean, with the service and all. Was he fitting in? He never did, you know. Never, never, except with you boys, and you all had to practically adopt him to get him through life here. His father was a big nincompoop, you know."

I almost laugh there, but smile politely instead. "I did not know that, no. But you should know that Rudi made a magnificent Marine. He was so good I am certain he was going to make a career of it after the war was over."

This, now, is the thing that really appears to strike something in her. She had the scone up to her open mouth when I said that, and then let her hand drop back to the table with it.

"*Career,*" she repeats, rolling her eyes upward in wonder. "I never even thought, not once, to connect that word and my boy."

I feel a bit lighter, more useful here, to have inadvertently tapped this source of badly needed good feeling.

"You would have connected it if you saw him there. A career, a career officer, probably, was where he was going."

I am being a little reckless with the language here, but it is recklessness in a good cause. Rudi's mom appears light-headed with the image she has of him now, and that is as good as we could ever hope to get it.

"Thank you, Morris," she says, holding her hand out regally and letting it hang there for me to do something with. Knowing well this is a once-in-a-lifetime arrangement, I kiss her hand.

Beck's parents have apparently been standing as silent witnesses to all this because when I rise, Rudi's mom gestures toward them, off a few feet behind me. She releases me to go to them and begins repeating all I just said to my mother as she sits down with a plate.

"We can't really stay longer," Mrs. Beck says to me, kissing my cheek and rubbing my arm gently.

"We just wanted to make sure we got a chance to say hello to you, son," Mr. Beck says. "How are you holding up? Are you okay? Anything you need, anything we can do for you while you are here? I can only imagine the strain of all this on you, you being the only one able to be here out of all you boys."

"You were always a very special group," Mrs. Beck says. "Always meant a lot to Beck, and he wasn't shy about saying so."

Were? Are? What is this thing now?

"That's why he's over there right now," I say with both a smile and a slight recoil, knowing me and my pledge are responsible.

"No," Mr. Beck almost snaps at me. He does point a sharp finger into my chest. "Whatever you're thinking, don't. It didn't take any kind of pressure or pledge to get Beck to do what he thought was right, and nobody could talk him out of anything once he had decided."

I nod enthusiastically, and Mr. Beck releases me from the lance of his finger. He could not be more right about this.

"Well, anyway, I'm good, folks, thank you for asking. I mean, this is hard, don't get me wrong. *Hard*. But I already feel like I'm getting through it, just as of today, really, you know?"

"Of course," Mrs. Beck says. "That makes all the sense in the world. I only wish we could see Beck, look at his face up close and see him like we are seeing you, so we could tell for ourselves that he's doing all right."

"He is," I say reflexively. "I can tell you he is. He's Beck, and Beck will always be all right, more than anybody I know."

I notice them leaning in tighter to each other as we get to this point. They smile gratefully at me but there is a flicker of something else there, too, and now I'm going to hear about it.

"We know," Mr. Beck says conspiratorially, and my knees almost give out with the shock of it. I am certain that my face goes bloodless because of the worry I see on theirs.

"Oh, dear," Mrs. Beck says, and rushes to give me a quick reviving hug before stepping back to her husband's side. "You don't need to worry about it. It's between us. Beck told us, in the few minutes we had on the phone, how Rudi died right there in your arms, with the two of you holding him."

Mrs. Beck loses out to tears here, and Mr. Beck picks up the baton of the conversation. "It is a wonderful thing, in the midst of this wretched, horrible thing, that you boys were there in his last moments. There is a rightness to that ending for that boy."

I am shaking with the bone-closeness of this conversation, and with some anger at Beck for not giving me a heads-up. Though, with me in transit since then, I don't see how he could have. But he *should* have.

"He tells us everything." Mrs. Beck sniffs. "That's how he is."

Not everything, I'm thinking. Not anymore.

"And Ivan—" Mr. Beck says before I rudely interrupt.

"Was already gone," I say, speeding things to a conclusion of my choosing. "We were all there, briefly, all together again. It wasn't much. But I was happy to be able to do my part. . . ."

To get them together.

I must look to the Becks like one of those wackos they say more and more of us look like when we come back from Vietnam. I am staring at the floor to stop all the motion, all the dizziness that is overcoming me as I remember it was my pledge that got everybody committed to the war in the first place, and then it was my nagging that forced us all into the same place for that last time.

"We just wanted you to know," Mr. Beck says close to my ear as Mrs. Beck presses close to my other ear. They don't try and force me to look up again. "Know that we know, and that if you need to talk to somebody, just to get it in the air, confidentially . . . well, you are our son, too. You all are. Come to us any time. The door will be unlocked."

I get kisses on both cheeks at once and they are all that is holding me upright until I feel a strong grip on my arm.

I look up to see the Becks waving and backing away quietly as The Captain asks as well, "How are you holding up, Morris?"

I shrug. "Just about?" I say.

"Well, if you've got a minute, I'd like to talk to you in my study. Won't take long, I promise."

I follow along to The Captain's study, which sounds like a nice seafood restaurant rather than the gallows it feels like right now.

It turns out to be neither, of course, but a small

musty-warm room with a handsome collection of military books and models, framed citations, and photos of The Captain over the years meeting some of the legends of warfare history, including General Patton. It also contains Ivan's brother, Caesar.

"Hey, Caesar," I say, shaking his big hand.

"Hiya, Morris, how are you?"

I've decided to go with "Fine, thanks," now, and for the foreseeable future.

Caesar has grown, quick and strong. He has always been about as close as it would be possible to get to a second Ivan, in terms of disposition and general Ivanness. In my absence, he has begun to look the part. He would definitely win the role of Ivan's stunt double in the unlikely event of him going into the movies and the even unlikelier event that he wouldn't do his own stunts. Caesar is rugged and ready and if anything maybe a little bigger-boned than his older brother.

The Captain takes a seat behind his desk and starts nervously playing around with the brass replica Sherman tank sitting there.

"I'll be direct here, Morris, because I know you've probably already had your fill of questions."

"Oh, no, sir, not at all. I understand why everybody has so much they want to —"

"What do you know, Morris, about Ivan?"

He did say direct.

I get all panicky, look to my right, to Caesar, who stands more or less at attention along with me, then back to his dad.

"Sir?" I ask, to play for time as much as anything.

"He's missing, Morris," Caesar says, because he's possibly the only person who finds The Captain's approach too meandering.

"What?" I say, astonished.

The Captain waves both hands in a crowd-calming gesture.

"Caesar," he growls. "No, now, it's not as official as all that. What it is is that, we cannot make contact with him. When we all heard about Rudi, through official channels, and then you and Beck were in contact with your families, we waited to hear from Ivan. Then, when we got nothing, that sounded strange, and so I have been trying since to get ahold of him with no luck."

It goes without saying that The Captain is not a worrier, and his composure remains ironclad now. But the fact that I am in here at all, that I have an audience with the great man himself in this room I have *never* seen the inside of in all the time I have known this family, and that the meeting includes the number-two son and nobody else, puts this at a level of need The Captain does not have to spell out for me.

"Sir, you know how he is," I say.

They both roll out a similar-sounding, utterly Bucyk chuckle at all of us knowing how Ivan is. It is quite welcome but not quite enough.

"It's also in the nature of his job," I say more helpfully, "and the nature of *this* war." I take the liberty to punch that emphasis there to assume just a small bit of authority on a subject where this man is otherwise the unquestioned authority.

The Captain nods at me, thoughtfully, appreciatively. I feel like I am being taken seriously, treated with a level of respect that I would never have earned with the man without my tour of duty in the hellishness of the Mekong Delta.

"I do understand," he says, "inasmuch as anyone can understand without going there himself. But I do have an abiding interest in the situation . . . and pretty soon I will have two." He nods in Caesar's direction.

"Yes, sir," Caesar says to me with familiar moxie. "As soon as I'm old enough, I'm signing up for the Army. Hope me and Ivan will be fighting together soon enough."

"That would be nice," I say in response to his eager-scary grin. "Not nice for the Vietcong, of course . . ."

"Gentlemen," Mrs. Bucyk calls while knocking at the door, "people are leaving now, and I think you want to be out here."

"Out here" sounds good to me. Out *of* here sounds even better.

"Okay, Hannah, we'll be just another minute," he calls. Then back to me. "I do get all that, Morris, and true, he will probably just materialize in his own good time. I also appreciate that you have a lot going on, and you can hardly be expected to bear all of the —"

"We really appreciate you even being here," Caesar adds.

"Certainly," The Captain says. "We absolutely do. But it just feels . . . not quite right. After all the years of you boys being together, and then not hearing from him nor being able to locate him myself. It may just be my overdeveloped soldier's sense of wariness . . . but you saw him, right? You were all together, just before Rudi got killed."

His overdeveloped soldier's sense of wariness is right now frightening the daylights out of me, and I am praying for Mrs. Bucyk's knock at that door again.

"Yes, sir," I say.

"So, nobody has spoken to him since then," Caesar says. They make a good team, these two.

"You were the last," The Captain says. "How was he?"

Oh, the question. Such a question. So many different ways to look at it, and to answer it, honestly.

"Fine, sir. He was fine."

"Really," Mrs. Bucyk says, bursting through the door. "Enough. Out here, all of you, now."

"You're right, Hannah, you're right," The Captain says, getting sharply up from his chair. She holds the door for them for good measure as first her son, then her husband file past.

"Sorry, Morris," she says, patting my back as I pass.

"Not at all," I say, "really."

I am the last person to leave, and I feel like part of a POW swap when Caesar finally opens the front door for me. I told Ma to go ahead in the car taking Rudi's mom home earlier, and the truth is the promised aloneness was heaven on the horizon in my eyes.

I stand on the Bucyks' porch, just like that last night after our going-off-to-war dinner with the haircuts and everything. Just like that, except for the many profound differences.

We buried Rudi today. He was killed by friendly fire, the friendliest fire of all time, and only the three of us know the truth.

Ivan and his rifle have not been heard from since.

Beck is on duty, and I can hardly fathom his being there while I'm back here.

And I am, indeed, back here, waiting to find out what the big wheel spins for me next. Or maybe I shouldn't just wait.

"What is the word on your next posting?" Caesar asks, standing in the doorway with his parents close behind.

"Well, it was all seriously short notice," I say. "Everything in motion before anything could be planned."

"I'll say," The Captain says. "That would be a logistical migraine nobody would want."

"Yeah," I say. "So, my CO said my new orders would be mailed to me here at home, in a week or ten days, and to be ready to report within twenty-four hours."

"Kind of unsettling, not knowing," Mrs. Bucyk says. "They could send you anywhere, to be doing anything."

I nod, chuckling, but in a pretty humor-free way. I'm afraid.

"Well, they probably can't top where they've already sent me," I say.

"True," says The Captain. "But you know, I still know a few people across the services. If you think you need any help with anything, just let me know. Couldn't get you out of a tour, of course —"

"Nor *would* you," Caesar snaps.

"Right, but since you've been already . . . Stateside, I might be of help. Pals who fought together in the Big One, they're pals for life. So . . ."

"Thank you, sir," I say, waving and walking down the steps at the same time. "I'll keep that in mind."

"And if you hear . . ." Mr. and Mrs. Bucyk say at the same time, with the same ache, and I so desperately would like to help them if I could do anything about it.

"Of course," I say, picking up my pace down the path to the street.

It may have been easier if they'd kept me in Vietnam. Truly.

PART
THREE

CHAPTER TWENTY-THREE

Beck

Lately I find myself thinking more and more about how improbably close the four of us were for all those years. I spent roughly equal time in the company of Morris, Ivan, and Rudi as I did with the members of my immediate family. And I adore my immediate family.

The other three spent an even greater percentage of their conscious hours on friendship than on family. Rudi once suggested without a hint of a joke that we get a house together, just the four of us. We were around thirteen at the time.

Information was always a shared commodity. Playground rumblings or the international kind, gossip, facts, lies, rumors — all of it was passed, filtered, and processed among us as if there were never any original source beyond ourselves. And if the topic in question *was* one or more of ourselves, there was exactly zero chance we would have heard it from any fifth party.

Which makes the news from my father that much more jolting.

"Ivan is coming home," he tells me on the phone. It is the first time since I deployed that he felt he could not wait until I phoned him. So I knew as I picked up the receiver that it wasn't going to be chitchat, but this information still catches me off guard.

"He is? Hans, that's kind of shocking to hear. What's up?"

It's a poor connection, and in the interminable delay between question and answer, Rudi flashes through my mind. What does Hans know? My stomach gets the same feeling as when it suffers a sudden ten-thousand-foot drop in altitude.

"He was seriously hurt in fighting," Hans says.

"What . . . ?" I say while he is still talking. He tries rushing his answer to accommodate me, but we are compounding the delay, chopping up the conversation with impatience.

"Right," I finally snap. "I'm just going to shut up and let you talk it all out." I never snap at Hans. And saying *shut up* in our family is bad form on par with lighting a fart on fire at the dinner table.

The pause on his end is a little longer than the line delay requires.

"I do hope that is combat stress I am hearing, son, and not your new military-inspired style of address. Anyway, yes, Ivan was rather severely wounded but he is going to be all right. It took a while for word to get back because he wasn't with his own unit when it happened and communication got snafued. Then Ivan himself seems to have been in no hurry to call home. He got shot in the face, the neck, and the shoulder. He should recover just fine for the most part. But he lost an eye, and that's the main thing."

This should not come as such a shock. It is a war. All we ever do here is shoot at one another and chuck explosives every which way. The shock would be in *not* getting maimed and mangled at some point.

And yet, I am shocked. One might think I'd be entirely shock-proof in light of everything. But, for better or worse, I now believe I will never get there.

Ivan, out of service. Ivan, shot, taken down, defeated by an enemy not named Ivan.

Unthinkable, once. Like so much else.

If they ever get a tourism industry functioning here they should coin a slogan — *Vietnam, the country that really makes you think.*

"Are you all right, Beck?" Hans says after carefully calculating the reasonable reaction time.

"All right. Yeah. No, sure, I am, I'm fine. At least he gets to go home, anyway. Getting away from here is an unequivocally great thing."

"Indeed. Though I wouldn't imagine your friend Ivan feels quite that way about it."

My friend Ivan. The phrase slaps around my head like somebody's playing racquetball in there, and I can't even begin to catch up to it right now.

"Yeah, well, that's just tough for him. He's got no business here anymore and he needs to be home. He's a tough guy, he can adjust to anything."

Again, he lets the pause bleed out some.

"Tough, yes, I suppose so," he says. "You're sounding more than a little bit that way yourself, my son."

"Am I? I guess that's to be expected, to a degree, under the circumstances. I don't mean to be sounding coarse at all to you, though, Dad."

I hear it as soon as it floats out. I don't think I've called him that since fourth grade.

"Not at all," he says, upping the kindness level in his voice. "You don't need to be worrying about me. I just want to know that I don't need to worry about you."

I am getting the signal that my phone time is about up, but I still have the freedom to appreciate the blatant absurdity of those words. I cannot resist.

Laughing, I say, "Worry about me, Hans. Worry 'til your eyelashes melt off. Because if you aren't worrying about me in the middle of this traveling circus of morbidity that means you either don't love me or you're delirious. And you should leave the delirium to me for the duration."

After a deep sigh, he laughs — less than me, but enough.

"I suppose any other response from you would have been unsettlingly artificial, Beck. So, as you wish, I will redouble my anxiety regarding your well-being."

"That's the spirit," I say, and I really am out of time now. "Dad" — there it is again, weak, needy, probably worrying him even worse — "I have to go. Love to Muti and the girls. Not too long in-country now, then I'll be back, too."

"That will be welcome, son. You are the last one left over there, and now it is your turn."

You would think, with my grades, I could count to four. But it's only catching up to me at this instant.

I am the only one left.

CHAPTER TWENTY-FOUR

Ivan

I want to be here.

I signed up willingly and have had every intention of serving out my tour of duty to the last day.

This is stupid. A waste of talent and training. It's obscene.

I would be on the very short list of guys who have not been trying to get themselves sent home, and now they are forcing me out so they have to drag some scaredy-skinny chicken of a draftee over here to fight in my place.

Nobody has *ever* had to do my fighting for me. This is a disgrace. I've been queasy in my stomach ever since I heard.

"That's just the medication," the deadpan doc says after I make my last-ditch pitch to keep my job. "Your stomach will settle down on its own. When you're all settled in comfortably — at home."

I am getting dressed in my uniform for probably one

of the last times ever. It is my discharge day from the hospital in Saigon. They flew me down for surgery after they did what they could on the base at Pleiku.

"It's not even my shooting eye," I say. "I always just closed that eye when I sighted through the scope anyway. So, if you think about it, I might even be more efficient now, since I won't have to be bothering with that."

"You are a very funny patient," the doctor says without any indication that he recognizes any humor in me or anything else. I suppose he's in a particularly unfunny job, to be fair. I figure it must be frustrating to be working as a doctor in a place where pretty much everybody else's job is the exact opposite of yours.

Like my job was. And like the guys who shot me up and blew me completely out of the game.

A corpsman has arrived to drive me to the airport and my flight. I hate to say it, but a wave of fear sweeps right over me at the sight of him and all he represents at this moment. It doesn't matter, though. I have to go with him regardless.

"Lieutenant," the doctor says after I have thanked him and started walking away.

I turn back, and he hands me the small presentation box.

"You almost forgot this," he says. "That would be a pity, after all you had to endure to earn it. You'll want to show that off to everybody once you get home."

"Thanks," I say, and go back to following my escort out.

It's the Purple Heart. I open the box and stare at it during the ride to the airport. No offense to the fine and noble profile of George Washington there, but this is the loser's medal. The Not-Exactly-Red Badge of Stupidity would be a more fitting name for it since they're giving them out by the crateload here to every numbskull too stupid to crouch down under fire.

Doc said it would be a pity to leave it behind, which is kind of funny since it isn't anything more than the pity medal for getting yourself scraped up. As for wanting to show it off to everybody? Who is *everybody* now, anyway? If they want proof of how badly I lost, I'll just show them my face.

The jeep shudders to a stop outside the airport terminal.

"That was some quality driving there, my man," I say to the confused-looking corpsman. Then I reach over and slap the medal in its case onto his lap. "Keep the change, have a good war," I say as I roll in the direction of someplace else.

CHAPTER TWENTY-FIVE

Morris

I don't want to be here.

I wake up so certain in that belief it almost scares me. The whole time in Vietnam I was like everybody else, yearning to be back home, in my good life, with my good friends.

And yet, I wake up to a crisp and sunny autumn morning — the kind I used to look forward to all the rest of the year — feeling like I don't belong here. I have walked around and around the town, rode trolleys and buses to the places I knew would put the old life back into me only to find that, one by one, those places absolutely failed to do anything like that.

Home is recognizable, but life is not.

Not only are my friends not with me, they are in places — dead in the ground or living in hell on earth — that make me feel so guilty for being home that I worry I'll go crazier here than back in the war.

One thing I have decided, one thing I can do for

myself, is I can stop waiting passively for word of an assignment. I have to talk to somebody. A Navy somebody, even if just to talk to a Navy somebody and stop listening to myself.

So, I dress under the old familiar Richard Petty racing poster, next to my little-boy bed, and I set out to see the somebody.

I ride the Green Line trolley into town, and am suddenly aware of the deathly screeching sound the steel wheels make on the tracks with every shift and gentle curve of the route. Despite the fact that I have ridden these things ten thousand times over the years, I somehow have never been on one that made this ungodly, unbearable sound.

My stop is supposed to be Park Street, but by Arlington I can't take it anymore and bail out two stops early.

The contrast is extreme between the subway I leave behind, with the trolley still screaming in my ears, and the relative peace of the Public Garden and the Common. In the perfect fall air, with the sun splashing all over leaves that are just beginning to turn, I briefly feel like here is the thing that's been so lost since my return.

So I step lightly the first couple of blocks to the Navy recruiting station, where I have some questions to ask.

But before I get there, I reach Brigham's and I stop right there on the sidewalk, unable to pass.

There have been quite a few times that I was unable to pass a Brigham's before, and the situation was always resolved by getting a butterscotch sundae.

Just like the one I got the day Rudi accompanied me to this same station, when it all began. He got hot fudge, marshmallow, nuts, and multicolored jimmies. We sat *right there*.

It is so hard to be home. Boston's breaking me down the way that Vietnam should have, and it's all about the one guy who came home with me and the two who didn't. The thing is, this city is the place that I never felt alone, ever, and now it's the loneliest place on earth.

I force myself away, no butterscotch sundae, no looking back. The effort of it and the concentration required have me marching very close to military style as I come in sight of the recruitment office.

And the commotion going on out in front of it.

There are a dozen or so people walking around in a circle right in front of the place. They are chanting things and carrying signs that I can't read yet but I could pretty well guess.

Whatever it is, it's their problem and I don't need to pay it any mind. I keep up my marching until less than half a block from the office's door I become suddenly very interesting to some of the demonstrators. They shift up a gear from tired-looking windup picketers who weren't being noticed by anybody, to inspired and angry shouters who see in me their time to shine.

"Don't do it, kid," says a doughy blond guy who steps up and blocks my way.

"Kid?" I say, as there is no way this guy is any older than me.

"You don't want to do this," says a second one, stocky and pimpled and also crowding in too close. He is likewise not old enough to be lecturing anybody, and to be blunt about it, I'd be willing to stack my worldly experience against these two any old time.

The rest of the windups continue their circular picket pattern, and I see now that their signs are reasonable enough, with slogans like *Peace Now!* and *Everybody Home for Christmas!* I wouldn't argue with any of that, and in a different world I might even join them.

These two guys breathing my air, on the other hand . . .

"And how would you know what I do and do not want to do, would you mind telling me?" I snap.

"Nobody in his right mind wants anything to do with this disgusting war," the blond one says.

"Well you also know nothing about the state of my mind, either, now do you? How would you, right? How would you possibly know that? In fact, I don't think you know *anything* about *anything*!"

I am pretty sure of two things at this point. The first is that I am right about everything. The second is that I might be tipping my hand regarding the state of my mind.

Oh, a third thing. I don't care.

I give the first guy a shove sideways to get him out of my way, and then I'm faced with the second one.

"Come on, pal," he says. "You have no idea what the Navy is up to over there."

Of course. They think I'm here as a potential warrior, not a seasoned and still-active one.

"Oh, I don't," I say, sneering right in the oaf's ignorant face. "But you do." I give him the same sideways shove as the first guy, though it takes more effort this time.

I get a small nervous prickle up the vertebrae of my neck as I get him behind me.

I am certain this is a thing connected to my time over there, but I feel the chill of threat in time to whip around and find the guy coming up on me. He freezes. Then he looks past me and I check over my shoulder.

The peaceable types have stopped marching and are now staring at the two guys.

I go back to my business and enter the recruiting office.

"Good day, young man," says the bright and energetic junior lieutenant. At the sight of me in the small storefront office he is up and out from behind his desk like I am an old friend returning after a long absence. I suppose in a way I am, since this is the office where I originally signed on. But he wouldn't know that.

"Hello," I say, feeling likewise happy to make his acquaintance and shake his hand. He's as friendly a presence as any I've found lately, and the scene outside his workplace makes me suspect he feels the same about me. "How's business, lieutenant?"

"Ha," he says, gesturing at the steady circulation of people who disapprove. "It's been . . . a little slow, frankly. But you are here to change all that, am I right, sir?"

I love it when people who outrank me call me sir.

"Um, maybe. In a way, sure. That is, I'm sorry, I don't mean to mislead you, but I'm not here to join."

The starch just about comes out of his perfect white uniform. His voice loses its bounce. "So, then, what are you here for? There is only so much this office is equipped to provide in the way of services to the general public. Are you sure you wouldn't maybe like to consider the opportunities available in today's Navy? We do offer a surprising —"

"Sorry to interrupt, lieutenant, but it's probably important that I tell you, I'm not thinking of joining because I'm already in the Navy."

He scowls at me. "Rank?"

"Just a lowly seaman, I'm afraid, sir."

The chanting outside appears to get louder, but that's probably just the comparative silence in the room. The lieutenant backs away from me and sits on the edge of his desk.

"As an enlisted man yourself, you must be aware how difficult things are these days, in a job like mine. Between *these* people" — he gestures out his window — "and the . . . unpromising nightly news reports, seeing a fresh face come through that door is a happy event, indeed."

He looks deflated, and now I feel like I have another thing to feel guilty about.

"Sorry to let you down," I say.

"It's nothing. But can you tell me what you did come in here for?"

I had almost forgotten myself.

"Oh, right, it's a bit of a story. See, I'm getting reassigned. I am just back, short notice. I was a body escort for . . . a good friend of mine."

"Oh. I'm sorry to hear that. And so . . . hold on, you've done a tour already? You've been over? To Vietnam?"

"Yes, sir. And while my tour wasn't completely up, it was close enough, they decided I should just stay, and I would be notified of my new posting once it was all worked out. Like I said, it was all kind of rushed there when I left."

"Sure," he says, "of course. And, you would like me to do . . . ?"

"Well, I had a lot of time to think about things on the trip back."

"A time of quiet contemplation, I would imagine."

"Uh, contemplation, for sure. I might have been talking some, too. Anyway, I got to thinking that, if the reassignment hadn't gotten too far, that maybe I could come in and talk to you about, possibly, if there was any sort of process, if I wanted to go into a certain specialty or another. If there was, yeah, a process I could explore, through you."

He's looking at me very thoughtfully now, rocking a little back and forth on his desk. I doubt I'd get this much consideration if he were not short on applicants and with a surplus of time on his hands.

"You know, I have never faced this situation before, so I honestly don't know. Might depend on what kind of needs there were in the track you were aiming for. Have you got —"

"Mortuary services, sir."

That, as you would probably guess, is a bit of a showstopper.

"Mortuary . . . ?"

I nod, almost afraid of hearing it come out of me again.

He nods in return, pondering my words, and me.

"I should gather, then, from this, that your journey transporting our fallen comrade from the battlefield through our system and on to his place of peace, included some positive experience?"

I have just a little bit of trouble answering him right away, as I revisit the details in my mind.

"Yes, sir, you could say that. You could possibly say, even, that I felt like that was the area of the service I would be most likely to contribute something of value."

The peculiar result of what, I have to confess, sounds even to me like a most peculiar conversation, is that the lieutenant smiles almost as winningly now as when I first walked in.

"Well, seaman, I do believe this is the first time anybody has come in here and done a selling job on *me*. It would be terrific if we could find the ideal situation for every potential enlistment. Now, there is a designation of mortuary affairs specialist, but frankly, since nobody has ever inquired about it before, I am without any hard information about it. Then, there's the particularities of your own enlistment situation, meaning you have come in here and presented me with two complete firsts in one day. So, why don't I get all your relevant information, and you take my card, and let's see if there's anything I can do for you."

"Great, lieutenant. That's great. I appreciate you even looking into it."

"Well, don't get too excited until we figure out how I'm going to get my bonus paid out of this deal."

He reads my stupid expression. "Oh, relax, will you. Jeez, you Nam vets really are tense, aren't you?"

"Hey, I'm easy," I say as he circles around to his desk chair and fishes through some papers to get my details down. "You should see the rest of them."

"Yeah," he sighs wearily. "Lucky for me I only normally see them on the way in, and not on the way out.

And lucky for you, you came through it all just fine and dandy."

I take the paper and start giving my name and phone number, home address, serial number, and service details.

"Lucky for me," I say. "Fine and dandy."

Not sure if I would ever want to say it out loud to anybody — except probably Rudi — but as I leave the office with Lieutenant Francis's card in my pocket, I feel elated about my prospects in mortuary affairs.

"Now, where were we?" says the stocky guy right in my ear, bringing my spirits back to earth.

"You did not sign up, did you?" the smaller guy says.

The even, rhythmic chanting of the larger group behind us sounds almost soothing, despite the words being, "Say it ain't so. Please don't go. Say it ain't so. Please don't go."

"It's none of your business what I did, so get lost."

"This is everybody's business!" the stocky guy with the iffy skin, and now the angry, red complexion, yells.

Then some demonic middle-aged spirit possesses me and I come out with this:

"Get a job, you lazy, privileged punk. Then you won't have all this time to bother real people."

I am about equal parts embarrassed at that and kind of pleased, leaning toward pleased, as I march along and away from this. Until it is his turn again, and he is most definitely following me this time.

"Yeah, but when I do get a job I won't be working for the United States Military Monster, destroying an innocent country for no reason at all!"

I turn crisply back toward the guy and we are together in two seconds. I take a big swing and feel my hand crackle as I connect with his big stony temple.

"You have no idea," I shout as he recoils and reaches a hand up to the spot on his head, "no idea whatsoever what we all have been through, fighting for *you*!"

I notice a couple of women break off from the group and rush toward us with their signs falling to the ground. "Stop, stop!" they yell, distraught.

"I knew you were one," the smaller guy calls. "I just knew it. You stink of death."

"Yeah?" I holler at him. "Well you just stink, period. And you did not know, because you know less than nothing."

The other guy has straightened up, and he pulls sharply away from the protest women who have grabbed his arms to try and stop him from coming at me.

"Right," I say, raising both fists and bracing for

him. I feel right and righteous in what I am doing. I feel like I am, in some strange, small way, fighting for us, for the four of us as well as the thousands of us who mostly would rather be home but are doing our bit anyway and do not need to be fighting a whole other depressing and demoralizing fight against knownothing fathead idiots like these guys, who are probably just covering up their own shame and cowardice by fighting one skinny sailor instead of the Vietcong like I did and Rudi did and Beck and Ivan are still doing.

Thuump.

He clocks me one mightily, right on the point of my chin. I see it coming all the way and still can do nothing to stop it as it lands and buckles my knees. I keep my legs under me, line up, and swing at him a little wildly.

Thuump.

He's got me square in the mouth this time, and I feel my legs giving up as I reel backward and he follows me to swing and connect one more time, bang in the mouth again, as I complete my fall onto my back and his meaty momentum carries him forward and down and crunching on top of me.

He's mouthing stuff at me that I am not comprehending and I am mouthing stuff at him that I am not comprehending, as the women and that other guy and now more protesters come to pull the guy away and I blink a bunch of times to make out what I am seeing and I take some small victory to note he is looking disheveled and demented and drooling with rage as they hustle him onward down the road and the demonstration itself breaks up and moves on.

I did something, though. I made a point of some kind. I defended an honor.

It wasn't all for nothing. It couldn't have been.

There is a cold cloth pressed against my mouth and I am getting assisted to my feet.

"Let's get you cleaned up, there, sailor," Lieutenant Francis says as we walk slowly back to his office.

"What am I doing, huh?" I say, holding the cloth to the split lip, the wiggly teeth. "Even when I'm armed, I'm only a little bit dangerous. I don't know why I let myself get involved."

"You're probably too noble for your own good," he says, pushing the door to the office open and holding it for me.

"Ah, you could be right about that," I say.

The lieutenant turns out to be pretty handy with the first aid. Between a small basic kit he has in the office and a cup of ice from a bar with no sign a few doors away, he's got me to the point where I can walk the streets without stepping on my own lip.

"Probably a borderline call whether that lip could use a few stitches inside," he says, sizing me up when I practice standing.

"I'm sure it's this side of the border," I say. I have a bloodstained gauze bandage in one hand and the cup of ice in the other. I move my jaw from side to side a few times. Hurts some, and makes a grinding sound back there, but I don't think it's anything significant.

"Keep at it with the ice for a while when you get home," he says.

I nod, raise my icy cup in gratitude. "Thanks for helping me out," I say.

"Thanks for standing up for the Navy," he says.

I am laughing on the way out, feeling the lip tearing a bit. "If the Navy needs me to stick up for them, I think they're in trouble."

"I respectfully disagree. I'll see what I can do for you on that posting, Morris. And I'll let you know as soon as I have anything for you."

"Thank you, lieutenant. I'll be waiting."

More anxiously than ever, since I now feel a little worse about the ol' hometown, and a little better about the Navy.

At first I cannot believe my mother's subdued reaction to my banged-up appearance. Maybe I look better than I thought.

Or possibly that's not it.

"What?" I say as she stands there over the telephone table, all fidgety.

"Ivan," she says, and accidentally pauses for breath long enough to freak me right out.

"Ma?"

"Sorry, Morris, he's going to be fine. He's injured. He's coming home. For good."

For good.

And I thought a fat lip was going to be the topic of the day.

CHAPTER TWENTY-SIX

Beck

Hey Morris Man,

There everybody was, all our lives, thinking I was the bright one. Bet you're laughing big about that one right now. You were positively genius in working it out so you got yourself sent home at precisely the right time. This place, old pal, is going out of its mind even more than ever before. Guys are so sick of the stupidity and pointlessness of almost everything we do here that they've started just refusing, flat out, to fight. No joke, the grunts are basically at war with the officers because the officers we're left with are morons and they simply do not care how many enlisted personnel get killed when they're sent out on search and destroy. Sometimes it's individuals, and sometimes whole units have started to just defy orders. And a lot of the time when they do go out, they're just faking it anyway. They don't really search for anything, and they engage with trees and bushes, shooting them up and even calling in close air cover — meaning me — to come in and blast away at enemy fighters who aren't there. The war was always stupid, Morris, but now it's STUPID. It would be a great laugh if it wasn't a greater tragedy.

So, let me ask you, oh wise Pledgemaster, how did I wind up over here, BY MYSELF???

I do trust you have heard that Ivan is coming home.

I will not lose my mind here, Morris. I won't. It is the only thing I have left, and I will protect it at all costs. Shall I tell you what that involves at this point? Yes, I shall tell you.

I rebelled, myself. Or partially, anyway, which I think was pretty magnanimous of me. Yes, sir, I told my commanding officer, the loathsome Captain Gilroy, that I was an engineer and if he gave me any more orders to man a machine gun I wasn't going to do it. What do you think of that? Didn't think I had it in me, I bet. I didn't think so myself. And I told him he has a very good engineer in me as it stands so let's not jeopardize that. Felt pretty good.

I don't know what that's going to cost me, pal, but I am keeping an eye out. He's not a nice guy, and he's a lifer, and the fact that he didn't say anything at all when I was insubordinate probably means he is in calculated-revenge mode. Maybe he's just glad I didn't kill him, which a lot of guys are doing to their officers now. And, since we are basically just going back and forth between riding in on bogus support missions on the one hand, or blasting the heck out of encampments of peasants who don't do anything for the "war" effort other than pad our body-count totals, maybe he just doesn't want to call any more attention to what we are and are not doing.

Maybe if I get away with it and he doesn't do anything, I'll see how far I can push it then.

I won't shoot him, though. Probably.

First thing I'll do when I do get home is I'm joining up with those Veterans Against the War people and I am going to protest everywhere and scream my lungs out about how wrong this all is. It will be like therapy, maybe.

Are you worried about Ivan coming home? Are you going to talk to him? I wish I were there with you. This is one thing we should be together

for, and that feels like my duty more than anything else right now.

Even if I don't know what I would say. Kind
of felt like we had plenty of time to think
about it, didn't it? I imagine, with him coming
your way, you're not feeling that way at all
now, huh?

Back to my sanity. I am also writing. Yeah. I
sent a couple things to the alternative answer
to _Stars and Stripes_ here, called the _Grunt Free
Press_. It's full of very funny and irreverent
stuff about what it's like here for the forces
in-country. Loads of made-up stuff, but all
totally true, if you know what I mean. The first
thing I wrote for them is good for a laugh,
though if my CO reads it I'm not sure he'll see
the comedy. I could be in some hot water. Though,
it's pretty unlikely he would read it.

There's a second piece I sent in, too, Morris.
It's not so funny. You'd be interested in it, though.
If they run it I'll definitely send you a copy.

I can last another month-plus in-country,
right? Smooth sailing after that. Sure, I can
make that.

How about you? Any word on your next assignment? Maybe you'll get something cushy, huh? And close to home. That would be nice, wouldn't it? Anything will be better than this scorched pit of despair, anyway, won't it? How's home? I miss it badly.

Sorry you are on your own for now with The Situation. What will you do? Any thoughts? I don't even know what to tell you, and when was the last time that happened? Right. Things aren't at all the way they are supposed to be, are they?

Take it easy, old friend. Write back soon. I need it more than I used to.

Peace.

Beck

P.S. Rudi has been making me cry lately, like, out of nowhere. I don't care for it, frankly. If you have any clout there — and I bet you do — tell him to knock it off. Rudi-spirit-goof.

Rudi

Boo!

Ha-ha.

I got my eye on you.

Ivan

The Army for some reason sends me home on a commercial flight, Pan Am, right out of Tan Son Nhut Airport in Saigon. From there to Honolulu I experience the most luxurious conditions I have ever imagined. The hostesses could not be nicer, and the plane could not be more comfortable. I am offered any food and refreshment I could want, and the other passengers are the most fun bunch of fellow travelers you could hope for, probably since they are mostly US servicemen on Pan Am's R & R service to go and let their hair down for a few mad days. Though by Hawaii they are mostly gone.

Even on the next leg, from Honolulu to LA, I am treated to full first-class service. I don't expect I will ever see the likes of this again, since I surely won't ever be able to pay for it.

I don't know why they gave this to me or who arranged it. Maybe it was a thank-you parting gift or a no-hard-feelings or something.

It was a great gesture, whatever it was.

And an awful shame of a waste.

By the time I land at the airport in Los Angeles, I am more tired and weak and anxious than I was on that truck convoy in Pleiku.

I ate nothing, did not sleep. I only grunted whenever the poor soul next to me tried to say anything, and to make it worse I kept climbing over him to get to the bathroom to look at the remains of my face. As if it were going to be changeable, like the weather across all these time zones.

I am in the bathroom at the airport now, and still nothing has changed.

It is a mess. There is a bandage patch where my eye used to be, and below that is a very obvious divot that represents the exploded bone structure under the skin. They tell me there are several surgeries ahead for me and that the staff at the VA hospital on South Huntington Avenue are going to ultimately be my closest buddies.

I don't know about that. I think the face I am looking at is the face I am supposed to have. It's the face I deserve. Every time one of those pretty and healthy Pan Am ladies looked at me I must have seemed like a stupid dog in a lightning storm, trying to burrow my way into the nice upholstery of the nice ride home the Army got for me.

What did I do? Lord almighty, what did I do, and where am I going?

I cannot go home. I cannot do that.

My connecting flight to Boston is boarding now.

I got the face I deserve.

Where is everybody? Where is anybody?

Why am I alone? Did I do that? Was it me?

Was it you?

No.

No.

No.

I hear a last boarding call and then another last boarding call for all passengers flying to Boston. Guys come in and go again and it gets busy but this is *my* sink. And then it gets quiet again.

Boarding is now closing for Boston.

I turn the water on in the sink all the way, and I wedge my big awful aching skull down in there, and I let the cold water run over my scalp and soak right on into my head and freeze it to the point of nearly tolerable numbness.

Then I turn off the tap and I straighten up and look at myself, with my hair slick and forehead streaming with the runoff.

I reach up, and I pick at my oversize eye patch, and pick at it some more, like picking a scab that isn't quite ready to come away just yet. But too bad.

The glue is quality, I will give them that. But it cannot hold forever. Here it comes now, pulling away with great reluctance but giving in, giving up, and I see the skin try to hold on and the wounds start weeping where the eye certainly can't, small oozings of blood tears, from the crescents of cut and patch and stitch and someday scar, and finally, the patch is up over my eyebrow, and it is off, and I am who I am now.

Rudi

Don't.
Please.
Don't.

Morris

Hey Beck Man,

   No. Don't see how far you can push it. Do not. You're almost home. I have your DERUS marked right here on my calendar, and it is so soon. Then you'll be back stateside in some easy egghead job, because they won't waste a big melon like yours. Then before you know it, your ETS will have arrived, you'll be a civilian again, and it's hello University of Wisconsin–Madison. Where you belonged all the time anyway.

   I am really sorry, Beck. It was the worst pledge ever. If I pledge not to make any more pledges, will you behave yourself and promise to keep from doing anything rash over there?

   I know it must be hard for you, that stupidity makes you mental and stupidity in war is like oxygen. But you have to do it anyway, or else I'll be forced to come back there and slap you around.

   I'll wait 'til you finish laughing. Okay, there now.

   The truth on this end is, I don't have any idea what to do. I'm terrified that Ivan is coming home. Not that he'll hurt me or kill me — which he might well do — but because it was different before. Him coming back means The Situation (good name, by the way) is coming back with him. That's what it feels like. He's not back yet, which is kind of weird since I thought he was coming last week. But nothing is truly weird now, is it?

I can't even look at people. Except for the funeral (you missed a swell time there, pal), I have been avoiding everybody like I'm some kind of rat that just wants to scurry around the base-boards and sewers without looking up at any humans at all. Even my own mother, who has been great but is going to start asking uncomfortable questions if I don't get out of here soon.

What were we thinking?? That this didn't happen? That it would just fade with time or stay in Vietnam and never have to come home with us and we could all be the same ever again, everybody except Rudi? What? Beck, what?

If he walks in that door right now I have no idea what I will say or do. I mean Ivan, of course. If Rudi walked through I'm pretty sure I would have a heart attack and die. I suppose that will probably be it if either one of them walks in, actually. Though if they both walk in together, maybe things will start looking up.

So, as you can see, old pal, you're not the only one who is capable of losing his mind. Yours is a better quality mind, though, so yes, do whatever it takes to maintain it. I like the sound of you writing for *Grunt*. That's a great idea, and of course they will take everything you write and I can't wait to see it. How much are they going to pay you? This could be your big break. Though if you write about any of us, you better be sharing the loot.

I wouldn't want you to become one of the protesters, Beck. I hope you don't do it. We'll just leave it at that for now.

As for my next assignment, I don't know for sure yet, but it's coming. As a matter of fact I am on my way out right now to a meeting I have with the recruiter downtown. I went to see him last week to ask him some things and check out some options. He called me back yesterday to say he has some information for me but wouldn't talk about it on the phone. So, I was heading out when your letter came and I couldn't leave without writing you back (ya big baby) and so now I have.

I think it's cool you're a big baby, though. I consider that a good sign, and I will write as often as it takes to keep you from going nuts.

Don't go nuts. I'll write to you again as soon as I know anything about anything. About anything.

Your pal as long as you don't protest against me,

Morris

CHAPTER THIRTY-ONE

Beck

"Beck! Beck, do you hear me? This is the straw, Beck! This one is the straw!"

Captain Gilroy is always talking lately about this mythical straw and what is going to happen to some poor camel because of the straw and what I am personally going to do with it.

Of course I can hear him. I'm just too busy to respond at the moment.

"You can see; I know you can see as plainly as I can!" I am shouting into the ear of one of our two gunners pouring heavy, brutal fire from the Spooky's machine guns into a human ants' nest of a village that is plainly no threat to anybody.

"Not now!" the gunner shouts, in a less-sure voice than he usually shouts that at me.

"Exactly now!" I yell. "If not now, when?" I am shifting around, monitoring the work of the gunner firing from the weapon mounted at the wide-open cargo door. From here, you can see the whole picture as we circle around and around the same "target."

"Beck!" Gilroy hollers. "Final warning. Knock it off now, or else!"

Or else. Or else what? What could get worse than this?

"There is not a single weapon down there, and you know it," I buzz into the gunner's ear. "Nobody is shooting at us. Look, there, on the trail back to base. There's the unit that called us in. Nobody's shooting at them, either. They're out on a picnic. Nobody's even playing the game. We're murdering numbers, man. We're killing people so that when it's all over, Gilroy gets to be a colonel!"

I notice off to my left the second gunner stops suddenly.

"Yes!" I shout. "See? Hear? It's only us shooting. Shooting for nothing."

The third gun keeps firing. It's remotely operated by the copilot up front, but I almost feel I could reason with the gun itself if I could get to it.

The firing from number one gunner stops and starts intermittently. He's testing the air.

"See? See? Guys, we don't have to do this. We have a choice."

The great miracle is that the third, remotely operated gun has gone silent.

This, this is a beautiful thing.

"Watch out!" number two gunner screams at me
just before impact.

It feels like former Pats linebacker Nick Buoniconti
has drilled me right between the shoulder blades with a
helmet-first tackle. My spine crunches and I am ham-
mered to the metal floor before I can even manage to
get a partial look. I writhe around and find the copilot
on top of me, then choking me, until I black out.

CHAPTER THIRTY-TWO
Ivan

I'm sitting on the porch.

For crying out loud. I have been sitting on my own front porch, unable to make the next move, after making all the thousands of previous moves that have brought me here.

Here. I am only here because of them. I had decided I was not going to come home, ever. That was it. I took the Greyhound bus route all the way across the country, which is not at all the swift form of travel the name would suggest. I didn't think America had as many towns as I stopped in between the Pacific and Atlantic coasts of this massive and awe-inspiring place.

And I wasn't done yet. I was back in line, in the station here in Boston. Everybody was staring at me, just like everybody in Arizona did, and Kansas, and Ohio, and New York, and just like everywhere I'll go in the future.

The future. It was going to be someplace north. I was still making up my mind on that, hoping, really, that when I got to the front of the line something there would make up my mind for me. And it did.

The lady in the ticket office who did not stare at me was what did it. Not that she was so great, because she wasn't; in fact, she was an old crab, and the only reason she didn't stare at me was because she didn't look at me at all, just like she didn't really look at any of the other people in the line.

And she didn't look up at her manager, who came by just as the long-haired stinker in front of me finished up and walked away with a ticket for whatever greatness awaits his smelly self in Montreal.

"Can you give me an extra two hours today?" the manager asked in a voice too young and too intimidated to be managing anybody, and surely not this somebody.

"No. Leave me alone, twerp," she snapped at him without a second's consideration before moving on to me. "Where you wanna go?"

The wounded and overmatched manager looked in my direction when I couldn't help a laugh. When he saw my face, or what there still is of my face, he looked quickly away from both me and the ticket lady, muttering as he left, "I told you to stop calling me that, Hannah."

Hannah.

Why did she have to be Hannah?

"I said, where you wanna go?" Horrible Hannah said as I started walking away from the desk.

I just kept walking as I heard her turn the question on the next person in line.

Where do I wanna go? I don't know.

Where do I have to go? That is at least answerable.

I need to go home to Hannah, who is in no way horrible, and to Roman and to Caesar. I couldn't not see them even if I don't want to *be* seen.

I hear my Hannah, my mom, let out a scream to make the ears of God bleed, from inside the window that looks out onto the porch. I brace for what's next as the thunder of many footsteps comes toward the door and toward me.

I wonder how frequently she has been pulling back that curtain to look for me.

The door flings open and before I can even get to my feet, my brother, Caesar, tackles me sideways, rolls me over on my back and kisses my forehead about a million times. I am starting to laugh when Mom follows, weeping and wailing, "Where have you *been*?" and the depth of the sadness of the sound chases away any thoughts of laughter.

I throw Caesar over, which is a lot harder than it used to be, and jump up to wrap up my mother as tightly as I can. "I'm sorry, Mom," I say, as I will undoubtedly say every hour for the rest of my life. She hugs hard for several seconds and then pushes me back to get a better look. She is crying rainbows of tears already, but then she sees my face, takes it all in, and goes from all melted melancholy to . . . crying harder still, only now with the most earth-shattering smile anyone has ever produced. And still more crying.

"Do you have any idea . . . ?" she says as she pulls me into a hug that has the cartilage between my ribs crackling loud enough to be heard by all the neighbors undoubtedly now at their windows.

"I'm so sorry, Mom, I really am," I say as I look beyond her, to the remaining parent. The one who is not crying and will never be crying. Except that . . . aw, cripes.

"Dad, please," I say when I see the unseeable. "Please, I'm begging you. I'm here now, and everything is fine."

He stands his ground and sniffs and refuses to

acknowledge the two, maybe three tears that have slipped down his face, and I can see the intensity there, the concentration that makes me believe if there is anyone who can *will* three tears to get right back into those ducts where they belong, then Roman Bucyk is that man.

"Where have you been, Ivan?" he says when Mom finally releases me. I walk up to him in that doorway, meet him face-to-face, man-to-man, and allow myself to fall into his arms, and he allows me to allow myself.

"I took the long way home, Dad. I needed the time. That's all."

I can feel him nodding even without seeing it. Even though that is not all. Not all at all. And we both know he knows it.

"We have company," he says as he puts me at arm's length, nodding at me like a coach putting a little kid into a big game.

"Aaarrrggghh" is by far the best I can do.

I feel Mom's arm around my waist and Caesar's hand squeezing the back of my neck, guiding me into the house behind Dad's lead. I guess they think I need complete manual control now.

But that's okay. What I am more keenly aware of than anything is that none of them made any kind of deal, big or small, about my face. And I don't mean out of politeness, either, because I know them and it is not that.

It's as if they don't even see anything but me.

"You went and put your eye out," I hear as soon as we hit the dining room. Then I nearly back out again as Rudi's mom comes to me, open arms. "I always told my boy it was gonna be him, and who ever thought it would be you?"

I can't even feel it as she hugs me. I look straight up at the ceiling, my mind trying to float up somewhere above this, my body going numb.

CHAPTER THIRTY-THREE

Morris

Hey, lieutenant," I say cautiously. I have been wary since he couldn't talk details over the phone. Like when you have some fatal condition and they make you come into the doctor's office so trained professionals can treat you when you faint onto your face.

"Good to see you, Morris. Jeez, lighten up, will you? Your lip seems to be healing nicely. It's a lovely day outside, not a cloud or a protester to be seen. Haven't seen those guys since that day, in fact, so I believe you scared the pants off them."

"Did you call me in so you could ridicule me in person, sir?"

That doesn't quite scare away his smile. "Wow. You are quite the serious fellow today."

"Sorry. I just have a lot of . . . stuff, that's all."

"Fair enough, but I have some *stuff* that might improve your outlook. I've been in contact with all the relevant people and the story is this. There is, in fact, a mortuary affairs specialty track."

"Great," I say, feeling indeed better already.

Lt. Francis shakes his head in wonder. "I still can't get over this enthusiasm for the subject. But, there's always got to be a first time for everything, right? And any man's enthusiasm for a job has to be a good thing in the end."

"So, when do I start? Where do I report? This is great. I'll go home and get my stuff right now and be ready to ship out —"

"Whoa, whoa, whoa, we have to slow this down, here. It is not — as you should know well by now — as simple as that with *anything* in the Navy."

Of course it isn't.

"Right," I say, straightening up in my chair and folding my hands on his desk like a good, attentive cadet.

"First thing, great thing, the men in charge have agreed to go along with your wish to proceed into mortuary service."

"Excellent. When do I start? Where do I report?"

"Morris . . . ?" he says, folding his own hands on his side of the desk and waiting for me.

"Okay," I say. "Sorry. Proceed."

"Thank you. The big thing is, this will require retraining."

"Sure," I say.

"All of the military mortuary training, including the Navy's, comes under the jurisdiction of the Army. Quartermaster Corps."

"Army. Sure, fine."

"That's JMAC, the Joint Mortuary Affairs Center at Fort Lee, Virginia."

It is killing me. I have become so certain that that is my place, in the war, in the military, in the universe, so certain that that is the closest I will ever come to making everything up to Rudi and all the Rudis everywhere and coming to some kind of peace with myself, that this has to happen, no matter what. Even if it means training with the Army.

"Yes, lieutenant," I say. "I am happy to do the retraining. Sign me up."

"It's three months of training, Morris."

"Okay, fine."

"It's 'okay, fine' with you, but what about the Navy?"

"What? What do you mean?"

"That is a big chunk of your remaining enlistment.

What's in it for them to train you and then get only a few months back, when they could just stick you in some crap post doing some crap job since you are already committed and have nothing to say about it?"

This is sounding heavy all of a sudden. Stupid of me, thinking it was as easy as that.

"What do they want?"

"You have to extend."

My heart enlarges, then contracts, then goes up into my throat and drops down into my stomach.

"How long?"

"One year."

I go stiff and silent but not by design. The thought has me all tied up. Noticing this, the lieutenant fills in some of the space.

"Including at least six months back in Nam."

CHAPTER THIRTY-FOUR

Ivan

I'm surrounded. Ambushed. This is the end, lonely friend.

"Go on, open it," Dad says.

I don't want to open it. They have to be able to see my hands shaking. *My* hands. Steadiest, deadliest dead-eye shot in the Army, and my hands are shaking just holding my mail. If it can possibly get any lower than this then I do not want to find out.

"Dad, I am so tired, it could actually be brain damage. Can't this just wait?"

He goes from excited to deflated in the time it takes me to form that sentence. I feel the stare of Rudi's mom's two eyes on the mangled side of my face even though I don't exactly have the peripheral vision to see her. I turn to see her reading over and over again the letter she received on her son's behalf from the USMC.

Purple Heart *and* Bronze Star. A glorious end, my friend.

"Ivan," Mom says, reaching across the table and stilling my hands without calling attention to the nerves. "The *Citizen* reporter is going to call back. You don't have to stay up for that. We just want to have at least something to tell him, that's all. Your father was so proud, but embarrassed not to be able to tell him anything."

The military information offices, in their desperation to put out any feel-good stories from the stink heap of feel-bad stories the war is generating, leaks partial information to local papers. They know about medals and citations as soon as they go out, but they don't know specifics until the families themselves reveal them.

"Congressman O'Neill wants to come and have a big public presentation ceremony, for both of you together," Rudi's mother says, voice cracking over there in the blackness of my vision.

I am on the verge of being sick if I do not get away from these decent and deserving people gathered around this table.

"Come on, hero," Caesar says, getting up and circling behind me from the blind side. He claps both hands on my shoulders, and I buck violently in my seat. I make a sound that I barely recognize but is something like sick, something like one of those Asian jungle tigers. My brother pulls right back away from me, and I tear into the envelope.

"There," I say, laying it on the table in front of me. I read the first lines:

The president of the United States takes pleasure in presenting the Distinguished Service Cross to Ivan Bucyk, Second Lieutenant, United States Army, for extraordinary heroism in connection with military operations involving conflict with an armed hostile force in the Republic of Vietnam.

The DSC. Second only to the Medal of Honor.

I already hear sniffles and moans when I pat the citation gently where it lies and excuse myself to go to bed.

It is no lie and no exaggeration to say that I am exhausted to a degree I have never experienced before.

It is also no lie to say I do not get one minute of sleep as I roll over and over and over again in my old bed in my old home that provides me no comfort now.

I wait and listen endlessly, like a sniper in the woods, until I mentally register company gone from the house and then each member of my family getting into bed.

Dad takes *hours*.

When they are all asleep, I get up, put on a new eye

patch, pack up my old pre-war duffel bag, grab a stack of my mail from the hall table, and head out.

"What are you doing?" my brother whispers, startling me as I turn the front doorknob.

"Gotta get away," I whisper back. "Going hunting."

"Let me drive you," he says.

"Gotta be alone," I say. "Not like I haven't hitched it before."

He is whispering the next round of this exchange I cannot bear, when I pull the door closed behind me.

CHAPTER THIRTY-FIVE

Morris

Once I have done it, I feel better than I have felt since probably the day before Rudi got his induction notice.

When Lt. Francis presented the options to me, I was stunned into silence and indecision. Told him I had to think about it. So I started thinking about it, about the options, about the life ahead. About being in Boston, or Virginia, or Florida or California or Maryland.

Or Vietnam.

About what I was going to *do* with myself, in the world, for my life.

By the time the trolley reached the station at Copley Square, I had no decisions left to sort through.

I jumped off the car, ran up the stairs, ran down Boylston Street to Tremont Street right back to a smiling Lt. Francis, who read my face with little apparent surprise.

"It occurred to me," I said with conviction, "you don't have to believe in the war, to believe in the guys."

"I'm going to get my bonus after all, aren't I?" he said.

This is how completely unglued the entire world has come lately: I am humming a little bit of "Anchors Aweigh" as I pack my bags to ship down to Fort Lee. I don't even leave for another couple of days, but I am that anxious.

It hurts a little to think about how much I want to get away from here, but that means I'll just have to stop thinking about it.

It hurts my mother more than a little. But when I explained how I feel about the good I can do in this job, she understood and even got rather proud of me. Then when I explained how the mortality rate in the mortuary services was almost zero, even in Vietnam, I could almost hear her humming "Anchors Aweigh" herself, though that could have still been me.

I know I'm doing a good thing.

And I know I'm running away.

Something spooky is transpiring, though, with Beck, in the way he seems to have uncanny timing with his correspondences to me. Not to mention the content.

When I hear the mail hit the floor I interrupt both packing and humming to go get it. There is a larger than usual packet from Beck, and I tear it right open.

It's a magazine. The *Grunt Free Press*.

It's, right off, a crazy-looking thing. The cover is all done in wavy-bubble psychedelic lettering with drawings of snakes and frogs in army helmets presenting the contents. I start flipping through and see serious articles like how not to catch a certain prevalent disease, and less serious ones like the methods career Army officers use to scratch their behinds with maximum efficiency. Each page looks like it is designed by a different person, some of whom could be university art majors, while others seem like kids going through fourth grade for the second time. There are poems and cartoons and photographs, and it is gripping stuff in some spots, boring in others, plain dumb in still others. But the overall tone is consistent: We are tired and frustrated and angry servicemen (mostly men), and this is our scream.

I already know I want to subscribe when I am back in Vietnam.

Page five, there is a two-column feature called "Grunt Speaks Out," with four individual, unattributed pieces all ringed in together by cartoon barbed wire.

One of the blocks of text is circled in green crayon, beside which Beck has written, *This is me!*

OUR LATEST OFFER

Step up, step up, Navies and Rentalmen, and listen to this latest and greatest offer on the table for all you in-country long-timers, short-timers, and out-of-timers.

Now and for a limited time only — who are we kidding, it's ALL limited time now — the officer class of the United States Armed Forces is offering an out-of-this-world, never-before-available alternative to absolutely every other option you have previously considered for getting your sorry government-issued self out of this stinking cesspit of a once verdant and vibrant land and back to your own cozy and familiar cesspit BACK HOME!

It's informally known as the Ho Chi Minh Discharge — and hold on, it's not one of those hideous conditions you've already caught over here but a legitimate(ish), tried and tested, foolproof (proven by actual, honest-to-goodness fools under laboratory conditions) method for being politely but firmly asked to (you'll need the John Wayne voice here, bless his leathery hide) get outta here, ya big monkey, and don't come back.

And it's even fun. All you have to do is get under the skin and up the nose and in the face and on the back of the next know-nothing, care-nothing, risk-nothing officer or NCO who tries to get you to do one more homicidal and/or suicidal absurdity in the name of duty to God and Country and to Mickey Mouse and especially to those hardworking peace negotiators who keep breaking off talks because they don't like their lab partner or the shape of the table or whether the doughnuts are filled with jelly or Boston cream, which isn't really cream in the first place.

So, friends, hurry to claim your very own Ho Chi Minh Discharge by rocking that boat, busting those chops, straightening down and flying wrong, or doing whatever else you can think of to do your part in pulling it all apart.

Because somehow they finally figured out that rather than have the malcontents gumming up the works here, it would be better to ship them back to those seats of wickedness like Stanford, or Boston University, or the University of Wisconsin–Madison, and see how they like it.

And remember, kids, if anyone says the word *dis-honorable*, you just smile and salute and shout out, "Thank you, sir, may I have another!"

I am shaking my head as I finish this perplexing unsigned thing and hoping that the other piece is going to be the "funny" one he referred to.

Then I flip to page twenty-three of the twenty-four-page magazine, where the entire page is one article and on it is written, again in green crayon, *This is me!* This one has a byline, though.

The Ghostwriter.

I know right away this is not the humor piece.

There is hardly a single person here with a gun who has not thought about using it on somebody he is not supposed to.

To kill.

But — to kill only part of that somebody.

To kill the part that is unrecognizable and wrong and new.

The part that is hateful and living like the river leech off the good and sweetest nature.

The part that was born in the conflict here in Vietnam and by all rights should die here. . . .

There's more. I read it through to the end, and by the end I am reading with the magazine pressed flat to the wall just to hold it steady enough to read it at all.

Then I crunch it up in my fist and run out the door. And run.

I knock and knock and knock to convince myself to go through with it. I am scared enough to wet myself as I stand on this old familiar porch and knock until somebody comes out here and deals with me.

"Morris!" Caesar says, sticking his big man hand right out and shaking my spindly one.

"Is he here?" I croak.

"Nope."

I am relieved and disappointed in equal, heaping measures.

"Where is he? How is he?"

Caesar whispers his answer heavily at me. "Starting with how, man, I don't think he is good in any way."

"I kinda figured that," I say. "Kinda feared it. So then, the *where* part?"

"New Hampshire. The shack. He's gone hunting."

"Ah, jeez," I say, feeling my slumping shoulders trying to drag me down to the porch and under it.

"Yeah," Caesar says. "I don't like it at all. I was thinking of driving up there. Whatcha think, you wanna come?"

I look up at Caesar's strong, young, eager, and familiar face.

"Sure," I say, "why not? Like I haven't been shot at enough already, right?"

"You are a funny guy, at a good time," Caesar says, punching my chest and sending me back a few steps across this porch in a way that makes me nostalgic.

"You sure you don't want to see my folks before we head out?" he asks as he pulls his car out of the driveway.

"I'm very sure. I mean, I would love to see them, but not 'til I see your brother. I just can't."

"That's cool," he says. "I get that."

As Caesar's very seasoned old Rambler Classic station wagon opens it up on Route 93, a blast of black smoke trails behind us, making it look like we are a spy car trying to lose a pursuer. I'm not sure we are going to make it to the New Hampshire state line, never mind the hunting cabin another three hours beyond that.

"This machine going to make it?" I ask.

He laughs. "I'll trust the machine, and you trust me."

"That'll work, I suppose. I remember when this car was your brother's."

"I remember when it was my parents'."

"I remember before that, when it belonged to the priest who died. I think it was still brown, before the paint faded."

I'm looking at the upholstery, the split down the middle and the tape failing to cover up all the white stuffing. The rotting floorboards look like they are just reinforced cardboard.

"Was it friendly fire, Morris?"

I nearly slip through the floor to the road speeding past below.

I don't know if I could speak if I wanted to. I know I don't want to. I stare in the driver's direction, and he looks at the road as he talks.

"You were there. And Beck was there. Rudi died *in your hands*. Ivan wasn't there? The sniper? He was there, and then he wasn't there? And now he's —"

"Ivan wasn't there," I say with a lot less horsepower than the brownish, smoky Rambler.

Caesar nods, pulls his lips tight.

"I love him anyway. I love him no matter what, and I'll love him forever."

It's a very long and very quiet journey the rest of the way. I could recite the entire *Grunt Free Press* from memory by the time we stop on the dirt track that leads to the little cabin with the big man in it.

I am so terrified of sneaking up and setting off bad things that I start calling his name out when we are still several hundred yards out. When we are seventy-five yards out, I get a response.

Bang!

A bullet cracks into a thin silver birch tree nearby, and I freeze where I am. I look to my side and see that if I reach out my right hand I can touch the wounded tree. I note as well that the slug hole is exactly at my eye level.

I turn around to face Caesar about five yards back.

"Think he meant to hit me?" I ask.

"Since he does still have one eye and you are still standing, I have to say no."

I walk back to him and say as big-brotherly and Ivanishly as I can muster, "I want to go in first by myself. We can't argue about it. He and I both need you to wait here. Please, Caesar. If I'm dead, then he's all yours."

Caesar is a good kid, and better trained at the concept of taking orders than probably anybody his age in the entire United States at this moment in our history. He remains rooted to the spot while I proceed toward the shack.

I am within thirty yards of the door when I step through the last thicket of trees, emerging from a natural doorway of two more silver birches.

Bang! Bang!

"You know full well how scared I already am without all that, Ivan," I call. "You could just clap your hands and achieve the same thing. Unless you just really hate birch trees."

His voice comes from inside the shack. "Did you come here to help me turn myself in, Morris, man?"

Did I?

"I still haven't exactly concluded for myself what I came for, Ivan. But that might be it, yeah."

"What if I resist?"

"Well, I don't believe you will shoot me. I don't believe you will shoot anybody today."

There is a long silence, but I don't have any pressing plans or functioning legs.

"What if I resist without shooting you?"

"Then I'll fight you, Ivan," I say.

I hear a big-bear theatrical laugh echo from the

shack. I believe I might even hear a smaller one come from a short distance behind me.

"I will," I say with some force.

"I know you will, pal. You'd fight anybody in the world if you thought it was for the good. Problem is, with Rudi gone there's nobody left in the world you could beat."

"Maybe you're wrong," I say, just to say something.

He lets out a smaller version of that laugh, then the front door of the place opens, and there he is. He is unarmed as he stands in the doorframe and waves me over.

There he is, and his eye isn't. His cheek is messed up, misshapen and discolored. He has a large bandage visible on the neck and shoulder area.

"Hiya, handsome," I say.

"Hiya, muscles," he says.

"Caesar is with me," I tell him.

"I know. I smelled the car about twenty minutes ago."

"Of course you did, hunter. Listen, I brought something else. I brought a message from . . ." My voice cracks as I pull the magazine out of my back pocket.

"An old friend?" he says, drawing the same magazine out of his.

Ivan walks right up to me, right up to me, and leans close with his magnificent mangled mug.

His forehead bumps mine, and it is only this instant that I can completely rule out the life-threatening headbutt.

"I'll be behind you, no matter what," I say. "We'll all be with you, no matter what."

He nods. And nods and nods and nods into my head, woodpecker communication, beyond words.

CHAPTER THIRTY-SIX

The Ghostwriter

. . . and your old hero Patton is here, and he says you're okay. Says maybe just a good savage beating would have done the trick, but shooting was effective, too. I needed something.

He says he forgives you. Your hero forgives you.

I forgive you, too. I forgive my hero.

And I'll be with you wherever it takes us, no matter what.

Love beats guns. Pals are pals.

And if war has an opposite, it's friendship.

About the Author

Chris Lynch is the author of numerous acclaimed books for middle-grade and teen readers, including the Cyberia series, the World War II series, and the National Book Award finalist *Inexcusable*. He teaches in the Lesley University creative writing MFA program, and divides his time between Massachusetts and Scotland.

YOUNG SOLDIERS ON THE FRONT LINES!

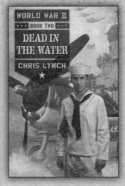

"All the sizzle, chaos, noise and scariness of war is clay in the hands of ace storyteller Lynch." — *Kirkus Reviews*

"A high mark for both historical fiction and rich, accessible storytelling." — *Booklist*

"Intense...A powerful taste of war on a personal level." — *Publishers Weekly*

SCHOLASTIC
open a world of possible

SCHOLASTIC and associated logos are trademarks and/or registered trademarks of Scholastic Inc.

scholastic.com

WWIICLEANe

SNEAK PEEK OF WWII BOOK TWO

CHAPTER ONE
One Torpedo

Every man should be prepared to lose one son in a fight to defend his own."

That is my Pop talking to me. To me and my brother, Theo. But that almost goes without saying. Naturally he is speaking to me *and* Theo, because the last time anybody said anything to me without Theo being close enough to hear every word was when I was one year old. Then he was born.

We're kinda close.

Anyway, that is Pop talking to my brother and myself as we stand in the front hall with the door wide open, the two of us just heading off to sign up to fight in the war that everybody knows is coming.

It is a shocking thing to hear, to say the least, on the way to do what we are on the way to do. It sounds like he is giving us up, throwing us to the sharks in the name of patriotism.

But of course he's doing no such thing. This, in fact, is Pop being as soft and emotional as I have ever seen him. He has more to say. The reason we have to keep standing there in the open doorway and wait for him to say the rest of it is because he is choking on that first part. So he starts again, but faster this time.

"Every man should be prepared to lose one son in a fight to defend his own. But no one should have to lose two."

Now it makes sense. Though, perhaps not to my mam. None of it makes sense to her. Which is why she is elsewhere today, bawlin' her eyes out to her own mam.

It is usually Theo's job to lighten stuff up when stuff gets all grim. And he is frequently kept busy with that task since my father, as fine and upright a man as there ever was, can also be the very definition of what is known as *The Dour Scotsman*.

"Ah, nobody's dyin', Pop," Theo says, laughing, waving our old man off and sauntering out the door. As if he thinks that will end it.

"Everybody's dying, Theodore," Pop intones — because that's what he does; he intones. He intones in such a tone, without even raising his volume, that the pavement shakes under my brother's feet and freezes him there as surely as if he'd been seized by the ankles.

"Sorry, Pop," Theo says, turning slowly back toward us.

"Don't be sorry, and don't be stupid. People are getting killed everywhere and every way in this bloody mess, and the surest way to join them is to go thinking that you somehow know something that the Brits and the Poles and the French and all those other sorry souls don't know. Do you know such a thing, my son, that you would like to share with the rest of the world before it's too late, if in fact it's not too late already?"

I believe there have been entire months during which my father has not spoken that many words.

"No, sir," Theo says, wisely. "I know no such thing."

Pop exhales then, releasing the lungfuls of air he had stored up in case more speech was required.

"Good," Pop says, softly. Then, he gets to his point-of-points. "Henry," he says to me, never much liking the nickname *Hank* outside of birthdays and holidays and such. "You're set on the Navy, correct?"

"I am, Pop."

He nods. "It's a fine and noble service." Pop himself sailed, fine and nobly, in the Great War.

"Me too, Pop," Theo calls out. "It's the Navy for me, too." It is a frantic attempt to head off what he knows must be coming.

"No, Son," Pop answers.

"Pop!" Theo shouts.

This would not be something my brother — or anyone else I know — would normally try on our father. I brace for the wrath.

But it doesn't come.

Pop shakes his head very slowly instead. He opens his mouth to explain, then looks down at his feet. He continues to look down as he speaks, haltingly.

"One torpedo . . ." he says. "One. Just the one, and that's . . ." His head starts shaking again. Then his hands, until he balls them into death-white fists and knocks them against his thighs. "We could never bear that. Thinking about that . . . every day, every night . . . I've seen torpedoes, up close, and their work, up close. . . ."

"But the buddy system," Theo pleads. "We'll be able to look out for each other."

"He's not your buddy, Theodore. He's your blood."

Desperate, Theo tacks the other way entirely. "They'll never put us on the same ship anyway, Pop."

"Yeah," I say, but with a lot less emphasis, a lot less expectation.

Then, a little curveball. Pop starts laughing. He looks up, shows us his rare red-rimmed eyes, shows his deep-creased face and mouth stretched in pride and stubborn admiration. "If there was any way, you two would make it happen. If you made it as far as the recruiting office together, you would make it happen somehow, of that I have no doubt."

It is, in the combination of the words and the manner, the warmth and the threat, titanic praise from the titan himself.

And it is also, definitively, the last word on the matter. My brother and I will not be enlisting in the same service. The logic of the argument is almost certainly my mother's, the steely resolve my father's, the combination an irresistible force.

He puts a big gentle hand on my back, eases me out to where Theo stands mute, and shuts the door firmly behind me.

OKANGAN REGIONAL LIBRARY
3 3132 03809 6147